Rudy's Memory Walk

Books in

THE ROOSEVELT HIGH SCHOOL SERIES

Ankiza

Juanita Fights the School Board

Maya's Divided World

Rina's Family Secret

Teen Angel

Tommy Stands Alone

Tyrone's Betrayal

Rudy's Memory Walk

THE ROOSEVELT HIGH SCHOOL SERIES

GLORIA L. VELÁSQUEZ

PIÑATA BOOKS
ARTE PÚBLICO PRESS
HOUSTON, TEXAS

Rudy's Memory Walk is made possible through grants from the City of Houston through the Houston Arts Alliance and by the Exemplar Program, a program of Americans for the Arts in collaboration with the LarsonAllen Public Services Group, funded by the Ford Foundation.

Piñata Books are full of surprises!

Arte Público Press
University of Houston
452 Cullen Performance Hall
Houston, Texas 77204-2004

Cover illustration and design by Vega Design Group

Velásquez, Gloria L.
Rudy's Memory Walk / by Gloria L. Velásquez.
p. cm. — (The Roosevelt High School series)
Summary: As high school senior Rudy adjusts his attitudes toward the elderly when his senile grandmother has to move in with his family, his girlfriend encourages him to talk with a friend's mother who has similar problems with her own mother.
ISBN 978-1-55885-593-9 (alk. paper)
[1. Alzheimer's disease—Fiction. 2. Old age—Fiction. 3. Grandmothers—Fiction. 4. Mothers and daughters—Fiction. 5. Hispanic Americans—Fiction. 6. Family life—California—Fiction. 7. California—Fiction.] I. Title.
PZ7.V488Rud 2009
[Fic]—dc22 2009038234

∞ The paper used in this publication meets the requirements of the American National Standard for Information Sciences—Permanence of Paper for Printed Library Materials, ANSI Z39.48-1984.

Printed in the United States of America
September 2009–October 2009
Versa Press, Inc., East Peoria IL
12 11 10 9 8 7 6 5 4 3 2 1

In memory of Francisca Molinar Velásquez
1929-2007

ONE

Rudy

Dad never chills, he's always uptight. The minute he hears the door open, he's on me about his car. "Did you leave me some gas?" he asks as I walk into the living room. Mom, who is on the loveseat talking on the telephone, glances my way. There is a strained look on her face, like when Dad gets trashed with one of his *compadres.* Something's gotta be up, I think, handing Dad the keys.

"I put ten bucks in after I dropped Juanita off. Where's Manuel?"

"He's upstairs doing his homework."

He's probably listening to that awful music if I know my little brother. Miracle he's not on the phone with one of those girls that call him all the time. Man, I wish I'd had that problem when I was an eighth grader. He acts like Mr. Hot Stuff, spiking up his black hair like a porcupine. Thinks he's a little Usher. Mom says Manuel's a lot like Dad—that he was a ladies man when they first met in San Antonio. That he had all kinds of *viejas* after him because he resembled a young Emiliano Zapata with his piercing eyes and thick black mustache. Why couldn't

I have looked more like Dad instead of Mom's side of the family? Mom says I look like Tío Manuel with my flat nose and pudgy cheeks.

"Damn Republicans! More tax cuts for the rich," Dad complains in response to the latest report on inflation. Dad always watches the evening news before he goes to bed. You'd think he'd do something different, like read a magazine or lift weights, but no—Dad never changes his routine. He's like an alarm clock that is set to go off at the same hour each day. Boring, that's what I think of Dad's life. He gets up at five a.m., grabs his Thermos of coffee and the lunch Mom packs every night, then drives off to Laguna Garbage where he's worked for the past seven years. How he stands it, I'll never know. But like Juanita and Maya are always reminding me, without a college degree, it's the ranks of the working classes. *Ni modo.* All I know is I ain't cut out for college.

Just as I am about to ask Dad who Mom is talking with, she hangs up the receiver. Her eyes are moist, and her lips are pinched. "What's wrong, Mom?" I ask.

Wiping away a tear sliding down her face, Mom answers, "*Ay, hijo*. It's Amá. She's real sick." Now Dad takes his eyes off the TV while Mom turns to him explaining, "That was Manuel in San Antonio. He says they can't take care of Amá anymore, that she's gotten worse."

"And what are we supposed to do?" Dad asks, the tension rising in his voice. I think back to the argument I overheard the last time Tío Manuel called, insisting we bring Abuela to live with us.

Mom sighs, her voice unsteady. "Manuel said we have to do something. Amá can't live with them no more. It's scaring the kids, and Amá said she wants to come live with me."

"Why you? Why not with Mariana?" Dad asks.

"Because I'm the oldest, that's why. And Manuel said if we don't take her, he's gonna have to put her in a home. I can't let that happen to her." Mom's voice breaks, so I move next to her, placing my arm around her bent shoulder. "Thanks, *m'ijo*," she whispers as Dad rises from the couch, mumbling he's going to bed.

"Do we have to bring Abuela here?" I ask softly. "I know she's my grandma and everything, but where's she gonna sleep?"

Mom squeezes my hand. "*M'ijo*, there is no other way. You'll have to share your room with Manuelito."

Thinking about how crowded we're going to be, I tell Mom, "Manuel's not going to like it. I can tell you that right now." Forcing out a "Goodnight," I head for the stairway. I can hear hip-hop sounds coming from Manuel's room as I fling his door open without knocking. Manuel is standing in front of his closet door mirror adding more gel to his spiked hair. "Hey, turn that music down! Dad's already in bed."

A conceited smirk spreads across Manuel's face. "Cut it out, Rudy. You're just jealous. I don't know what Juanita sees in your pudgy face anyway!"

Smiling, I answer, "That girl can't live without me. Remember, if you need any advice about chicks, just ask King Vato here."

Now Manuel orders me out of his room, and as I shut the door behind me, I think about what Mom said, hoping she changes her mind. It'd be major torture sharing a room with that little punk.

In my room, I set my alarm for seven a.m., then I pick up my Cucaracha comic book, but all I can think about is Abuela having to move in with us. How I wish I had a cell phone so I could call Juanita and talk with her about it. Guess I'll have to wait until tomorrow.

The next morning, Mom drops me off at Discount Foods on her way to the Coral Inn, where she's been cleaning rooms for the past five years. Mom's one of the head housekeepers, and she's always going on and on about how clean they keep the rooms. Sometimes she brings home huge tips from all the rich people who stay there. One time some man left her a $50 tip. Mom was so excited that she couldn't talk about anything for months. If you want to know the truth, it makes me sick that Mom has to clean rooms for a living. Her back is always aching, and her hands always smell like cleaning detergent. But Mom insists the manager treats her really well and that it's way better than working in the fields. That's what she and Dad used to do in Texas—pick cotton. They moved around a lot, even went to Oregon until they finally came to California to work in San Martin. They ended up here in Laguna when Dad got on part-time with the garbage company.

I wave to Stella, the manager, as I shuffle to the back room to clock in. Next, I put on my apron and badge, walking back to the first cash register where Matt is already ringing up a customer. "Hi, Rudy. You're just in time," he says. I stare at the old man who is meticulously extracting a few dollar bills from his wallet to pay for his purchases. It takes him forever, but he finally hands the money to Matt. By then, I've bagged up his groceries and placed them on the cart. Following the old man out to the car, I'm forced to walk like a snail. And to top it off, it takes him just as long to open the car trunk.

"Thank you, young man," he says as I finish placing the last bag of groceries neatly inside.

"You're welcome, sir," I reply, pushing the cart back to the racks at the front of the store and thinking how I never want to get like that old man.

The morning goes by quickly as I bag up groceries for one customer after another, but for some odd reason, I keep noticing all the old farts and how they hold up the lines, frustrating the customers behind them. I wonder if that's how Abuela is going to be.

During my lunch break, I go over to the meat department to say hello to Mr. Cameron, Tyrone's dad. If it weren't for him, I wouldn't have gotten this job. Mr. Cameron put in a good word for me with Stella when they were short-handed, and the next day I got the job. Tyrone was real bent because he wanted me to apply at Inboxes where he works, but I told him I'd always wanted to work in a grocery store. Mom thinks its cool since I get discounts on some of the store items.

"How's it going, Mr. Cameron?" I ask, poking my head inside the double doors to the meat counter. Mr. Cameron pauses to gaze up at me. He's wearing a nylon cap, and his white apron is covered with red stains.

"Couldn't be better. Lots of meat to prepare. How about yourself? You and Tyrone staying out of trouble with them girlfriends?"

"Yeah, we're way cool with them."

Mr. Cameron smiles, and we talk for a few more minutes. As I return to bag groceries, I think about how angry Tyrone was when his dad took off, leaving the family alone. I'm glad Mr. Cameron returned home and that he and Tyrone are now getting along. My dad can be an idiot sometimes, but I don't know what we'd do if he suddenly left. By the end of the day, my arms are aching from bagging groceries, and I'm eager to clock out and hop on the city bus.

When I get home, I find Mom lying on the couch elevating her feet. She's watching the cooking channel. "Getting any new recipes from Rocko the Jocko?" I tease her.

"Today Rocchio is showing everyone how to make veal parmesan. How was work?"

"Good. Where's Dad?"

"He went to the junkyard with his *compadre.* Won't be home late."

"*Híjole,* I wanted to borrow the car . . . I'm supposed to pick up Juanita in an hour."

"Don't worry, *hijo*. You can use mine. The keys are next to my purse on the little table."

"Thanks, Mom," I tell her as she goes on to ask if I'm hungry, but I explain that Juanita and I are eating at Foster Freeze.

"*Qué bueno,* the cook gets a night off," Mom sighs.

"Isn't Manuel here?"

Mom frowns. "I told him about Amá coming to live with us, and he got pretty mad, said he was going to Jordan's."

"I knew he wasn't going to like it."

I hope the news doesn't make Manuel do something stupid with Cassie's brother. Jordan acts like a little hood, always getting into trouble.

When I pick up Juanita, I go inside to say hello to her parents. Mr. Chávez sternly reminds me to be back by eleven, but Mrs. Chávez is warm and friendly. She even asks if Mom is still working at the Coral Inn. Before we leave, Celia, who looks like she is ready to pop asks if I can let Mom know that she's looking for part-time work and that she cleans really good. But Juanita laughs at her, reminding Celia she's gonna have a full-time job taking care of a baby.

On the drive to Foster Freeze, Juanita says, "You know, if it hadn't been for Celia getting pregnant, Apá would've never seen how strict he was and finally let me date."

"Lucky for me. When's her baby due?"

"In May. That's all Amá talks about."

"Yeah, I heard there's gonna be a big *pachanga*, that's what Maya told Tyrone."

Now Juanita's almond-shaped eyes brighten like two full moons. "Yeah, Apá wants to roast a pig. Ms. Martínez and Frank are gonna be the *padrinos*."

"That's great."

At Foster Freeze, we get in line and when we finally arrive at the register, there is an old lady who asks for our order—only it takes her the longest time to write it out. We're even forced to repeat what we ordered several times, since she has trouble hearing.

Heading back toward a booth with our order, I confess to Juanita, "I don't know why they hire old people to work in fast food places. They oughta get rid of them."

"Rudy, that's mean. One day you're gonna be old too."

"Well I'm not gonna act like that. I can tell you that right now."

No sooner have we sat down than the old lady approaches our booth saying, "I forgot to give you your change. Sorry."

As soon as she's out of sight, I gripe to Juanita, "See what I mean?"

"What's bugging you, Rudy? Since when did you get this mean attitude toward old people?"

Feeling the heat from Juanita's gaze, I answer, "Ever since I heard my grandma's coming to live with us, that's when."

Juanita's face softens. "She is? That's really nice."

"You gotta be kidding! I can't stand old people."

"Don't say that, Rudy. My *abuelita* died when I was a little girl and I never got to know her. And Apá's mom died when he was a baby. You're lucky to still have your *abuelita*."

"That's what you think!" I reply defensively. "Manuel and I might have to share a room. There goes my privacy."

"*Pobrecito*," Juanita says sarcastically. "I've never once had a room all to myself. How can you be so selfish, Rudy? Think about all the families in California who live cramped up in apartments because they can't afford to pay rent—two or three families at a time."

"That's enough!" I say, reaching for Juanita's hand and kissing each one of her stubby little fingers until her frown is replaced by a smile.

After I take Juanita home, I think about what she said about me being selfish. Maybe Juanita's got a point. Yet I can't help but wish things could stay like they've always been at home.

TWO

That following Wednesday, we're in the middle of dinner when Mom announces, "Amá is coming this weekend. We're picking her up on Saturday at the Santa Barbara airport. Manuel, I need you to move your things into Rudy's room before Saturday."

Manuel lets his fork drop on his plate, making a loud clanging noise. "I told you I don't want to do that. Why can't she move in with Rudy?"

"*Estás loco*," Dad reprimands Manuel whose face is red from anger, his Zapata eyes bulging out of their sockets.

"Don't get so bent," I say, trying to console Manuel, who's been acting moodier ever since Mom talked with him. Still, I can't help but agree with him that the whole idea stinks. Why should we have to give up our privacy for some old lady we don't even know?

Manuel is livid. "Where am I gonna put all of my stuff, like my stereo, my CDs?"

Mom pats him on the hand. "*M'ijito*, I know it'll be rough, but there is no other way."

Abruptly pushing back his chair, Manuel is on his feet. Dad orders him to finish his dinner, but the next thing we hear is the banging of the front door as he storms out.

Disappointed, Mom shakes her head sadly and I tell her, "Don't worry, Mom. Manuel's just cooling off."

"Thanks, *hijo*," Mom says with a faint smile while Dad threatens to beat the crap out of Manuel.

I want to defend Manuel, to let Dad know that the whole damn thing is unfair, only I don't. I suck it all up for Mom's sake as we finish our meal in silence.

By Friday, I've rearranged my bedroom, and the minute Manuel gets home from school, I insist it's time to move in his furniture. "We can put your bed over by the closet," I offer, knowing Manuel will like being next to the closet door, since he gets off on admiring himself in the mirror.

"Gee, thanks," Manuel says, tinges of sarcasm in his voice.

Mom suddenly enters the room and offers to help, but Manuel snaps at her, so she quietly retreats back downstairs.

First, we move Manuel's twin bed alongside the closet. Then we bring in his small chest of drawers, which fits against the wall at the foot of his bed. By the time we finish moving Manuel's stereo and CDs, the room starts to look cramped.

"And you better not touch any of my CDs unless you ask permission," he warns.

"Don't forget to leave me a check-out sheet," I chuckle, hoping to defuse his pissy attitude. After all, if anyone should be upset, it's me. Not only am I the oldest, but I've had to get rid of half of my stuff just to make room for him.

After we're done, I help Dad set up the small bed for Abuela that Mom bought at a yard sale. Still, I can't help but feel resentful when I see how much more space Abuela will have while Manuel and I are cramped up like sardines.

On Saturday before they leave for the airport, Dad makes it clear that he expects us to be home when they return from Santa Barbara. Manuel leaves for Jordan's, but when he doesn't return in two hours, I call him, demanding he get his butt home. We play videogames for a while, and when Juanita calls to invite me downtown with her, Maya, and Tyrone, I explain that we're waiting for Abuela. Then I watch the Clippers game until I hear Mom and Dad pull up in front of the apartment. Hurrying upstairs, I holler at Manuel, "Turn off your music. They're here!"

By the time I get downstairs, Mom is walking into the apartment with Abuela, who looks way smaller and more wrinkled than the photograph we have of her in the living room. Abuela's wearing a flowery green dress with a bright blue jacket that hangs on her thin shoulders. Her face is a toasty brown, and her thin gray hair is pulled back in a bun.

"Amá , you remember, Rudy?" Mom asks in Spanish.

"Rodolfo, you're so big," she says, her Spanish accent sounding like Mom's. Moving closer to embrace her, I'm struck by a pungent smell of damp towels that have been hung out to dry.

Dad orders Manuel, who appears at the top of the stairway, to help me bring in Abuela's luggage. When we're done, Mom calls us both into the living room, where she and Abuela are seated side by side on the couch. In Spanish, Mom says, "Amá, this is Manuelito—he's not a baby anymore."

Wincing, Manuel awkwardly stretches out his hand to greet Abuela, who surprises him with an embrace.

"Now can I go?" Manuel begs as Dad enters the room with a large box, ordering Manuel and me to take Abuela's stuff upstairs to her room.

Following us, Mom tells Abuela that she has time to rest before dinner. And when we get to her new bedroom, Manuel rudely admits, "This *used* to be my room."

Mom glares at Manuel, but Abuela doesn't even seem to notice. Her eyes are dim, as if she's just awakened from a deep slumber. As Manuel turns to leave, Mom reminds him that dinner will be ready in an hour.

Back in my room, I pick up my new *Muscle Up* magazine, wondering what it's going to be like with another person in the apartment, especially some old lady who can barely make it up the stairs by herself. Does Mom think Manuel and I are going to babysit her or what? No way in hell, that's for sure, even if she is my grandmother.

Manuel returns just in time for dinner, and I can tell he's still upset when he avoids sitting next to Abuela. Instead, he sits by Dad, which he never does. Tonight we're having my favorites, meat loaf and mashed potatoes, so I forget all about bodybuilding as I serve myself huge portions. While we eat, Mom attempts a conversation in Spanish with Abuela about the family in San Antonio. "Does my *padrino,* Ernesto, still work for the city?

"Isn't Ernesto about ready to retire?" Dad adds.

But Abuela, who's looking spacier by the minute, doesn't comprehend the question. "He lives next to your cousin Mario. He's lived there since he was a little boy."

Mom and Dad exchange a quick glance as Abuela begins to talk about her *comadre* Marta, who lives down the street from her. After she repeats the same story about Marta's daughter, Abuela reaches for the salt shaker.

When she begins to salt her coffee, I can't restrain myself anymore. "Abuela, that's salt," I blurt out. "You want some sugar?"

Confused, Abuela sets the salt back down as Mom passes her the sugar. We all watch as she puts one, two, three heaping teaspoons of sugar into her coffee, and she's about to add more until Mom reaches out to stop her.

"I thought *I* liked sugar," Manuel mumbles as he rises from the table and exits the kitchen.

Abuela barely tastes the meat loaf, mixing it with the rest of the food on her paper plate until it looks like mush. But the minute Mom breaks out with the ice cream, Abuela smiles, happily eating every last spoonful until her bowl is empty.

After dinner, Abuela stays in the kitchen to help Mom with the dishes while I join Dad in the living room. When he turns the TV on to *Sábado Gigante*, I can't help but think this has to be the most idiotic show on Univisión. Tonight Don Francisco is wearing a bunny suit and he's hopping around the stage like an idiot. I'm relieved when the doorbell suddenly rings.

Juanita greets me at the door with a huge smile. "Surprise! Did your Abuela get here okay?"

"Yeah, she's here. Man, you sure look fine," I answer, running my eyes across her tight-fitting top.

"Cut it out, Rudy," Juanita scolds me as she steps inside. "Can I meet her?"

I give her a short kiss. "Are you sure you want to? She's a little crazy."

Just then, Mom and Abuela come walking out of the kitchen and into the dining room.

"Hi, Mrs. Ortiz," Juanita cheerfully says, turning to face them.

Mom smiles, introducing Juanita to Abuela, who tells Mom in Spanish, "She looks like Carmen."

Her dimples showing, Juanita shakes Abuela's hand. When she asks who Carmen is, I explain she's my Uncle Manuel's wife. Then Mom asks if we're going out.

Juanita answers in that sweet voice that makes me want to kiss her all over again. "I wasn't sure if Rudy could get out tonight since his *abuelita* just got here."

Her eyes brightening, Abuela says, "*Vayan a pasearse*." Mom and I glance at each other, surprised that Abuela has finally said something that makes sense.

Following Juanita outside to her Dad's old junker, she tells me, "Your abuela's sweet."

"Yeah, I guess, but she's way out there. Where are we going?" I finally think to ask, opening the door for her.

"Want to go to the Rialto? The new *Exorcist* is showing. It's supposed to be real scary. I guess Tyrone wanted to see it, so I told Maya if we could, we'd try to meet them there."

"Nothing, absolutely nothing could be as scary as living with my grandma!" I answer sarcastically, only Juanita doesn't laugh at my joke.

THREE

"That was a creepy movie," Juanita concludes as we file out of the theater and into the lobby of the Rialto with Tyrone and Maya.

"My favorite part was where the lady has the baby and it comes out all covered with worms," Tyrone says.

"Yeah, that part was cool," I agree, watching Maya and Juanita exchange a gaze of horror.

Heading toward the entrance, we wave to Tommy, who is waiting on a customer at the concession stand. Tommy's been working at the Rialto for several years now and sometimes he gets us in free. But not tonight. Too bad, since I'm almost out of money and I don't get paid until next week.

"Let's go get some yogurt," Maya suggests, leading Tyrone outside to the chilly night where the streets are bustling with college kids headed for their favorite night clubs.

"As long as I get home by eleven. I wouldn't want Apá to change his mind about letting me date," Juanita agrees as we turn in the direction of Yo Yo's yogurt shop, which is on the opposite side of Main Street.

"Don't worry. We'll make it back by eleven," I reassure her, wondering how Tyrone puts up with Maya's constant bossiness. She always has to make the decisions. Me? I like girls like Juanita who let a guy take the lead.

Tonight Yo Yo's is crowded, and it takes us forever to get through the long line of customers. Then we stand around and wait around for another five minutes until we're finally able to get a table, only it's outside, and we're forced to raise our voices over the rock sounds coming from across the street.

"Did you know Tyrone got a new car?" Maya asks, between mouthfuls of her peach yogurt.

"You got your own wheels?" I ask Tyrone, feeling instant frustration because I still don't have my own car.

"Yeah. My dad lent me some money so I could get it."

"Your dad's tight. It sucks having to borrow my parents' car all the time. Wish my dad would fork out some cash."

"Yeah, well, maybe it's Dad's way of not feeling guilty for what he did to us," Tyrone says, dark shadows lingering in his eyes.

"Don't be so mean, Ty," Maya groans.

Tyrone shrugs his shoulders slightly, then he explains how he was going nuts having to take the bus as well as hitching rides. "Now I'm even able to help Ray give the guys a ride home from the Teen Center."

"I don't know how you find the time to do all of that," Juanita sighs. "I thought senior year was supposed to be easy, but I can barely keep up with my assignments and still help Amá at home."

"It's all about time management," Tyrone brags.

"Now you sound like Mr. Grinde," Maya says, "but the truth of the matter is that you don't have to do housework like we do. That's why guys have more time."

Tyrone and I smile at each other as Juanita agrees with Maya. Then they go off into one of their "kick-ass feminist" discussions, which I can't stand if you want to know the truth. But Tyrone and I are already used to it, so we wear them out, inserting a few facetious comments about male chauvinism.

Once they've calmed down, Maya turns to me and says, "Heard your grandma's living with you."

Frowning, I say, "Yeah, she is, but she's some kind of psycho."

Juanita glares at me while Maya asks for an explanation. "She's crazy! She repeats herself a thousand times, mixes everything up. I think she's out of it most of the time."

Sounding like one of those lame reporters on the evening news, Maya says, "Maybe she's got Alzheimer's."

"Old timers—what's that?" I ask, trying to sound serious.

Giggling, Maya answers, "Alzheimer's, *tonto*! It's a disease of the brain. My grandma in New Mexico was diagnosed with it a few years ago, only now she's a lot worse. You ought to talk to my mom sometime. She knows more about it."

When Juanita seconds this idea, I say, "You've gotta be kidding! I ain't gonna tell nobody." Juanita reaches out and pinches me so hard that I almost jump out of my chair, saying, "Take it easy, girl."

"Don't listen to Rudy," she adamantly explains, "I met his *abuelita* today and she's real nice."

"You know Rudy . . . he'll do anything for attention," Tyrone teases as Maya repeats her suggestion that I talk with her mom.

We hang out at Yo Yo's until it's close to Juanita's curfew, then we say goodbye to Maya and Tyrone who are parked in the new parking structure. As we walk back to where our car, Juanita brings up the subject of Abuela again, making me promise that I will be nice to her.

Back at the apartment, I'm not annoyed to find Manuel watching music videos on the small TV he's placed on the top of his dresser. His eyes are glued to Beyonce, who is rhythmically swaying her sexy body to the verses of her newest hit song. As the song comes to an end, Manuel looks up and says, "I wish I had a cell phone. Even Jordan has one."

"Get a job first. Cell phones cost a lot. Besides, you'd be on the phone calling girls all the time."

Manuel grins, exposing the tiny dimple on his left cheek that he inherited from Dad. But his smile quickly fades. "I can't stand Abuela. She keeps taking my things. I told Mom, but she won't do anything about it."

Stretching out on my bed, I ask, "What do you expect her to do, kick her own mother out?"

"That'd be cool. Then I could get my room back."

I'm about to call Manuel a selfish little moron, but I don't. Deep down inside, I can't help but wish it were just the four of us again.

On Sunday, by the time I've showered and dressed, Mom and Abuela have already returned from church. Mom glances at me from the living room where she is engrossed in one of her *Healthy Living* magazines. I think it's a stupid magazine, but Mom always buys the latest issue at the grocery store. "*Hijo*, will you check to see if Amá is all right?"

"Yeah, sure. Where is she?"

"She went out in front for some fresh air."

As I step outside, I find Abuela on the front sidewalk bending down to look at something. Straightening out, she holds up a small rock. "See how pretty this is."

Nodding, I tell her, "Mom said for you to go in now."

"*Sí, hijo*," Abuela answers, bending down to pickup another rock and placing it inside the pocket of her sweater, which is already bulging with rocks. Then Abuela turns toward me, only she pauses as if she's confused and doesn't recognize our apartment.

I take her by the arm, saying, "This way, Abuela."

Just as we are about to go inside, a car honks, and I turn around to find Tyrone pulling up alongside the curb in a faded yellow Honda Accord. Closing the door behind Abuela, I walk up to his car, and Tyrone tells me to get in.

"Bad-looking car," I say, sliding into the front seat.

"Yeah, it runs smooth," Tyrone says, maneuvering the car back onto the street.

"I'm still saving up to get my own car this summer."

Heading toward the freeway exit, Tyrone asks, "You want to cruise over to Taco Bell?"

"*Órale*, only Juanita ain't gonna like it."

"Yeah, Maya would kill me if she knew. She says Taco Bell is the worst Mexican food ever."

"*Chale*—they don't have to know about it."

"Like I can keep a secret from Maya." Tyrone says, and I have to smile, knowing exactly what he means.

After we've stuffed our faces at Taco Bell, Tyrone takes me back to the apartment. Abuela is out front again, walking up and down the sidewalk searching for rocks.

"She really is crazy," I mumble to myself, wondering if I should take her back inside. Reminding myself that I'm not Abuela's babysitter, I decide to leave her alone with her stupid rocks.

FOUR

My first period class is U.S. Government, and today it turns out to be lively because the entire class gets involved in a debate about the war in Iraq. In the middle of Mr. Kenyon's lecture on The Gulf of Tonkin Resolution, which gave President Johnson authority to make war during the Vietnam era, Cindy Boyd raises her hand to say that her father said the United States has created another senseless war in Iraq, similar to the one in Vietnam. Before Mr. Kenyon can respond, Eli shouts out, "Somebody has to stop terrorists like Saddam Hussein!"

Then another classmate, Joan, who is across from him, says, "Eli, you're an idiot. My mom teaches at the university and she said the U.S. government helped put Saddam Hussein in power, like they've done with other dictators. And now we're trying to destroy him because it's not beneficial to us."

Mr. Kenyon attempts to intervene before the discussion gets more out of hand. "Let's not personalize the discussion. Let's stick to the facts."

Only it's too late. Several other students join in to support Eli's defense, saying they have family members who are proud to be in the military. But Joan doesn't rescind her remark. Instead, she turns to Mr. Kenyon and asks him point-blank to clarify U.S.- interventionist policies in other countries such as Nicaragua. Still hoping to temper the discussion, Mr. Kenyon directs the conversation back to Vietnam, clarifying that many historians have indicated that Vietnam was an unnecessary war.

"Yeah, like the one in Iraq!" Martín Gutiérrez yells, and the debate rips wide open again, only this time Mr. Kenyon is saved by the bell.

In English Lit, we're discussing Shakespeare, who might have been one of the greatest writers ever, but his English sure sucks. It's hard to understand, and then most of his plays have tragic endings. Me, I prefer happy endings like in the *telenovelas* Juanita's Amá watches.

I've almost zoned out of Mrs. Harrison's lecture on *Hamlet,* when Devon raises his hand and asks, "Is it true Shakespeare was gay?"

The room fills with giggles while Devon grins, pleased with the response.

Rina, who is directly behind Devon, slaps him lightly on the back and says, "So what's wrong with that?"

For once, I'm on Rina's side. Giving Devon a mean stare, I ask, "You got a problem with that?"

His cheeks reddening, Devon shakes his head. "I was just asking, that's all. I'm not homophobic if that's what you're thinking."

Mrs. Harrison moves to our side of the room and asks everyone to listen up. Then, her eyes meet Devon's, and she explains, "There have been many great authors who were gay or lesbian—Gertrude Stein, Oscar Wilde, and Virginia Woolf, to name a few."

Devon doesn't say another word after that as Mrs. Harrison continues her lecture on *Hamlet*.

As the bell signals the end of class, I file out the room with Rina. Flexing my muscles at her, I say, "You oughta take weight training, build up your muscles like mine."

"You're still a puny lightweight!" Rina laughs, turning to go in the opposite direction.

Hurrying out of the main building toward the gym, I head for the weight room, which is adjacent to the locker room. Once we're all suited up, Mr. Fawcet makes us run a couple of laps, and then we do our usual warm-ups. Chart in hand, I begin my training program, going from free weights to different stations where I keep track of my progress. By the time fourth period ends, I've almost completed my entire set of exercises for that day.

After Consumer Math, I meet Juanita at her locker. It's drizzling, so we eat in the covered walkway next to the science building. Within minutes, we're joined by Rina, Sheena, and Tommy. Maya and Ankiza have gone to a senior class meeting and Tyrone has already left for the day.

"Did you build up your puny muscles?" Rina teases, biting into her sandwich.

For the second time today, I flex my arm muscle at Rina. Everyone laughs when Juanita touches my arm and says, "*Ay*, Rudy, you sure know how to turn a girl on."

"You know it, baby!" I instantly reply, and there's more laughter, only I'm not joking. I'm dead serious.

Then Tommy brings up last night's Laker loss to Houston, and we're off on hoop talk until a frustrated Sheena flings her crumpled up lunch bag at me.

"Cut it out!" I holler, and Rina opens her big mouth to warn Sheena about my muscle power.

Sheena pretends to start shaking, so I warn her that she's beginning to look as ugly as Rina. But Sheena takes this as a compliment, smiling facetiously at me.

Sheena's always joking about how she's the only white girl in our group, but we tell her it's cool. Her Spanish has even improved, and sometimes she comes up with words in Spanish that we don't even know. But Sheena really makes us laugh when she repeats cuss words in Spanish.

Sheena's voice suddenly turns serious. "Rina said your grandma's living with you, that she's sick."

Before I can answer, Juanita adds, "Maya thinks she might have Alzheimer's."

Great, I think to myself, now it won't be long before the entire school knows about it.

"Ryan in my English class has Work Experience at the Oceanside Care Center. He helps out with a lot of old people with Alzheimer's. You might want to check it out," Tommy suggests.

"Why would I want to be around some more crazy people like my grandma?" I answer, wishing someone would change the subject.

"If anyone's crazy, it's you!" Rina chastises me.

On my feet, I raise my fists at her as if we're going to duke it out. Sheena joins in on the fun, putting her hands together as if she's holding a microphone. "Ladies and gentlemen, round three of *Lucha Libre*!" she announces as Rina rises to take several short bows. Now Juanita and Tommy start to applaud.

My last class of the day is Spanish, which I like a lot this year because we have a new teacher, Mr. Villamil, who is from Puerto Rico. After four years of taking high school Spanish, I finally get a native speaker for the advanced Spanish classes, although I still miss Mrs. Plumb. With her, a guy could get away with swearing in Spanish, and she never knew it—but with Mr. Villamil, it's a different story. Mr. Villamil is cool, though. He talks a lot about Ponce, where he was born, and Rina, who is also Puerto Rican, joins in to talk about her own Borinquen customs and traditions.

As soon as the fifth period bell rings, I'm off to Discount Foods, thinking how lucky I am to be a senior this year and be able to leave campus early. After I've clocked in, I retrieve my badge and apron from my locker in the break room. Then I go bag groceries at Myrna's station until it's my turn to do a store sweep. I really enjoy going up and down the aisles cleaning the floors with a gigantic dust mop. One time I found a $10 bill all folded up. Another time, I found someone's hearing aid. But today, there's *nada*, only dust and a few dead flies.

I'm cruising down aisle ten when I meet up with this old man who seems lost. He makes a complete circle, then stares at me helplessly.

"Sir, can I help you?" I ask, noticing the same confused look Abuela had yesterday when she was outside collecting rocks.

"I'm looking for Mother. I don't know where she is."

"Maybe she's in another aisle. Would you like for me to check?"

The old man's face crumples like an old newspaper and he begins to whimper like a baby. "We were supposed to go to church this morning." Then he turns and starts up the next aisle, calling out, "Mother, it's time to go."

I'm about to call the manager for help when a frantic sandy-haired lady appears in the aisle. Her voice is quivering, "Dad, I told you to wait for me in the car. You scared the daylights out of me."

"I was looking for Mother," the old man replies.

Taking him gently by the arm, she says, "Mom's dead. Don't you remember, Dad?" The old man doesn't seem to understand.

Turning to look at me, the lady apologizes. "Sorry. Dad has dementia. Guess I shouldn't have left him alone in the car."

"That's okay," I nod, not quite understanding what she means. Then, as I watch them leave the building, I think about Abuela, wondering if that's how she's going to end up.

FIVE

Professor Sonia Gonzales

It was a relief to have made it to the end of the quarter. Although I loved my students, it was nice to have a break from teaching classes and all those germs going around. It seemed as if lately all I did was catch colds, which made it even more difficult to make it through the ten-week quarter. Maya constantly teased me about all the different supplements Glenn had recommended I take. She insisted Glenn always looked as if he were on a supplement high. But I didn't let Maya's teasing bother me. After all, I knew how difficult it had been for her to accept my divorce from Armando, let alone see me with another man.

I was about to take the last sip of my mid-morning cup of coffee when the Christmas-like jingle on my cell phone went off. Answering it, my brother's rugged voice came through. "Sandra, you have to get out here. Mom was screaming her head off yesterday, and the neighbors reported her. The police came, they said she can't be left alone anymore."

I felt my neck muscles tighten like rubber bands. "What do you mean, the police came?"

"Just what I said. Mom wouldn't stop screaming. So the neighbors got scared and called the police."

"Didn't they try to help her?"

Robert released a frustrated sigh. "Yes, they tried, but Mom had all the doors locked and wouldn't let anyone in."

"I thought Tía Lola was keeping an eye on her?"

"It's been too hard for Tía Lola—sometimes Mom even tries to kick her out of the house, says she's not her sister. It's time to do something, Sandra. We need to find a place for her."

Closing my eyes for a moment, I was taken back to the year of my separation from Armando. The terrible fight with Mom that summer in Santa Fe when she'd kicked me out of her house. But later, she came around, even apologized. After that, we'd been closer than ever. "I don't want to do that," I finally whispered, my eyes moist.

Now Robert's voice grew agitated, "And you think I do? I wish Alicia and I could take her, but our place is small. And besides, she's never liked Albuquerque."

Robert was right. After Dad's death, Robert had begged Mom to move closer to him, but she wouldn't hear of it.

"Are you still there?" Robert asked.

"I don't know if I can go. I'm getting ready to give finals."

"Well, you have to—either that or they're gonna call Social Services and take her away. Is that what you want?"

It was just like Robert to make me feel guilty. If only Mom hadn't spoiled him so much, "*M'ijito* this, *m'ijito* that." It made me sick to my stomach thinking of the way Latino moms cater to their sons. After a very long minute, I said, "Let me see what I can do. Who's with Mom now?"

"Tía Lola said she'd stay with her until you got here. Call me as soon as you make the arrangements."

After we hung up, I burst into tears, wondering why Mom had to contract this terrible disease. She'd always been the strong one—the self-sufficient woman who could do anything, make anything. When I was a little girl, she made all of my dresses, knitted sweaters for the entire family at Christmastime. She'd even fixed Tía Lola's plumbing one year. Why Mom? I asked myself over and over until there were no more tears and I was finally able to clear my thoughts. Reaching for my cell phone, I located Glenn in his classroom where he was finishing up the last period of the day. Sniffling, I reconstructed my conversation with Robert and as I paused, choked up by tears, Glenn stated, "I'm coming right over."

While I waited for Glenn, I wandered aimlessly around the house until I finally turned on the TV, hoping to quiet my anxious thoughts. Oprah was featuring Marcel, her favorite decorator, and the room makeover feats he was able to accomplish in a few hours. Staring at Marcel's perfectly decorated rooms, I thought about Mom's life, wishing I could make it over that easily. Just then, I heard the front door open, and Maya sauntered into the family room.

"Getting any ideas?" she asked, slumping onto the couch. When I didn't answer her, Maya turned to gaze at me, her voice growing serious. "What's wrong, Mom?"

"It's your grandma in Santa Fe. She's very ill. Your uncle Robert called. He says she can't be alone anymore, that it's time to make some decisions."

"Poor Grandma," Maya whispered, adding. "I'm really sorry, Mom. What are you going to do?"

"I don't know," I whispered, blinking back the tears. "I can't seem to think straight."

"Want me to make you a cup of herbal tea? That always makes you relax."

"Thanks," I smiled, "but I called Glenn, and he's on his way here."

"That's good," Maya said, "But watch out, he might try to get you hooked on more supplements."

As Maya headed for the stairway suppressing a giggle, I thought back to the year I'd met Glenn at the campus coffeehouse. I'd instantly felt attracted to him. I was even more impressed when I found out he taught Spanish at San Martin High School and that he'd been raised with Chicanos in San Jose. Then when Glenn revealed that he'd lost his wife to breast cancer, I'd admired him even more. If anyone understood what I was going through with Mom's illness, it was Glenn.

By the time Glenn arrived, he found me sitting in front of the fireplace going through one of my photo albums. "That's a nice one," he said, pointing to a picture of Mom bending down in her backyard to water her flowers. Marigolds, petunias, sunflowers . . . Mom loved them all.

"I don't know what to do," I whispered, as Glenn gently led me to the couch. Leaning my head against his chest, I began to weep softly. Glenn stroked my hair gently, and after a few minutes, his jade eyes peered into mine. "Why don't I call the airlines and get you on the next available flight?"

"But what about my finals?"

"I'm sure you can find someone to proctor them."

"And Maya? I can't leave her by herself."

Reappearing at the top of the stairway, Maya said hello to Glenn, then earnestly argued, "Mom, I'm a senior now, I can watch myself."

Winking at her, Glenn continued, "Besides, I can drop by, make sure Maya's not having any wild parties!"

"Don't give me any ideas!" Maya shouted, and I forced out a smile.

Glenn spent the next hour calling the airlines until he found a flight leaving for Laguna the next morning and connecting through LAX to Albuquerque. The next thing I did was call my department chair to let her know that I would need someone to administer my finals.

After making a hurried call to Robert to give him my itinerary, I called my best friend Sandy to let her know about my unexpected travel plans. "Don't worry about anything," she reassured me in her calm therapist voice. "I'll call Maya tomorrow—maybe she'd like to have dinner with Frank and me."

It was almost midnight by the time Glenn left and I finally climbed into bed, only I couldn't sleep. I kept seeing images of Mom locked inside her house screaming wildly.

SIX

Professor Sonia Gonzales

Robert was waiting for me at the baggage claim area. There were more wrinkles on his broad face, and shades of gray around his temples. "Sonia, you look good as always," he said, embracing me. "How's Maya?"

"She's great. Excited about her senior year. "Where's Lily?"

Reaching for my suitcase, Robert explained, "She couldn't get the day off, said she'd call you later."

After graduating from UNM, Lily had been hired at the Salud del Valle Clinic that provided healthcare services for low-income families. Unlike Lily, who was dedicated to helping the Latino community, Robert was more preoccupied with buying cars and boats with his comfortable engineering salary.

"So how's Mom?" I finally asked as we stepped out into the brisk Albuquerque air and headed for the parking structure.

"She seems to have snapped out of it and hasn't tried to kick Tía Lola out anymore, but we have to do something."

"I know," I whispered wearily, remembering all the times Maya and I had begged Mom to come live with us. But she had always refused to leave Santa Fe. Now it was too late.

Minutes later, we were headed north to Santa Fe in Robert's new Explorer. Gazing out the window, I felt bewitched by the New Mexican desert landscape with its sagebrush and chaparral. It was no wonder that artists like Georgia O'Keeffe had chosen to live out their lives in La Tierra del Encanto. There was a definite spiritual energy that seemed to surround the quaint New Mexican towns that populated northern New Mexico. It was here that Rudy Anaya's Última and my own Navajo ancestors had gathered their sacred herbs, chanting prayers to the spirits.

Robert's voice brought me back to the present moment as he pointed out the new subdivisions on the outskirts of Santa Fe. "A lot of rich Anglos have moved here," he scoffed. "And they keep coming. Now there are new malls and restaurants everywhere you look."

"Too bad," I answered, wondering if like O'Keeffe, one day I would also return permanently to New Mexico.

Entering Santa Fe, we took the Sandía exit to the Mariposa area where many of the city's original Spanish-speaking families still remained, despite gentrification and the arrival of the wealthy newcomers. Mom lived in the same three-bedroom adobe where Robert and I had spent our childhood surrounded by family. Tía Luisa lived on the next street and Tío Jesús, Mom's oldest brother, lived several minutes away from the Guadalupe church plaza.

Mom and Tía Lola were in the kitchen drinking coffee when we arrived. There was a blank expression on Mom's face. "Hi, Mom," I said, embracing her. "I've come for a visit."

Smiling, Tía Lola said, "María, isn't it nice? Sonia came all the way from California to see you."

Fidgeting in her chair, Mom's face remained unchanged as I gave Tía Lola a hug. When Robert explained that he had to return to Albuquerque, Tía Lola asked him for a ride to her house, and Robert earnestly agreed. Before they left, Tía Lola led me into the bedroom where she handed me Mom's pills. "This one is the tranquilizer the doctor prescribed for when she's real agitated or hallucinating."

Suddenly afraid, I asked, "How will I know when that happens?"

"Don't worry, *hija*—you'll know."

After they left, I followed Mom into the living room, watching her turn on the TV to the afternoon cartoons. For the next hour, Mom giggled and talked out loud with the cartoon characters as if they were carrying on a conversation with her. Deciding Mom was safe for the moment, I went into the bedroom to unpack, but when I came back, Mom was in the kitchen trying to heat some leftover meat loaf in the microwave. She kept fussing with the different settings, but the microwave still wouldn't start. "Like this, Mom," I said, pushing the controls. Mom snorted in disgust, but I pretended not to notice. We sat down to eat, only the next thing I knew, Mom was spreading jelly on her meat loaf. "Mom, don't do that!" I protested, grabbing the jar from her hand.

Mom exploded with anger, her face was flushed when she screamed, "Get out of here! Leave me alone—I know what I'm doing!"

Mumbling an apology, I fled to the bedroom, wondering how in the world I was going to cope with Mom's irrational behavior. Tears began to surface as I thought back to all the beautiful moments I'd shared with Mom—my first communion, my high school graduation, the huge wedding with Armando that she'd helped plan down to the last detail. Even Dad's funeral had been a celebration of sorts with all of the family. Only now, Mom was gone and somehow I needed to accept the fact that she would never be the same.

That evening, I went to bed early, but all night long I heard Mom pacing throughout the house. At three a.m., I finally got up and very firmly insisted it was time for her to go to sleep. This time, Mom offered no resistance, meekly following me into her bedroom. While I helped her change into her nightgown, I glanced around the room, shocked by its unkemptness. There were piles of clothes on the floor, cardboard boxes filled with knickknacks, and even Dad's electric saw was lying at the foot of her bed. The closet door was open, and the closet was overflowing with an array of things that didn't belong there. I felt the tears welling inside me as I thought about the mother who had prided herself in being clean and orderly, the mother who had bragged about her spotless home.

The next morning, I awakened to find Mom in the kitchen where she was frantically removing dishes from the cupboards and placing them in paper bags. The table was completely covered with pots and pans. As she reached for the coffee maker, I lunged forward, taking it out of her hands. "No, Mom. I need it for my coffee!"

Her eyes narrowed. "You're not stealing my things, if that's what you think!"

"Mom, how can you say that?" I gasped. "I'm your daughter—I wouldn't steal from you."

Just then, I heard the front door open, and Tía Lola appeared in the kitchen. Mom turned to look at her sister, saying, "I want her to get out. She's trying to steal my things."

"*Cálmate*, María. Sonia is your daughter," Tía Lola said, signaling for me to get Mom's pills from the bedroom.

My heart pounding, I knew the time had arrived to make the calls I had been dreading.

That afternoon, I visited several different Alzheimer's care facilities in Santa Fe, but I couldn't help but feel repulsed by them. They were filled with elderly women who seemed like helpless rag dolls in a place that smelled like death. While each care facility had an outdoor area with flowers and benches, the locked gate and high walls reminded me of a prison. The only place I had remotely liked was the Sage Nursing Home. It employed two Spanish-speaking nurses aides and there was even a patient like Mom, a Mexican *viejita* who spoke Spanish. Another reason I liked the Sage Nursing Home was that the nurse in charge had gone out of her way to patiently answer all of my questions as well as describe in detail the daily activities they provided for their patients. Still,

I went away from there feeling guilty and confused. How could I imprison Mom with all those other rag dolls, take her away from the home she'd always loved?

Walking back to my car, I thought about Mom's brothers and sisters. Maybe the time had come for them to help out. Reaching for my cell phone, I dialed Tío Jesús. "*Hija*, you know my grandkids practically live with us. We can't have María around them. That would be dangerous," he explained.

Next, I called Mom's younger sister, Tía Marcela, but she was also apologetic, "I wish I could help, *hija,* but I don't have the time. I have my part-time job at J.C. Penney's, then I help out at the Senior Citizen's every Friday."

Disgusted, I drove back to the house, repeating Tía Marcela's final words in my head. "Can't you take her home with you?"

As soon as I walked in the front door, I described my dismal day to Tía Lola, ending with my plea for help to Mom's selfish siblings. "*Qué vergüenza*," Tía Lola said, shaking her head in disappointment. "If only my health weren't so bad."

We both gazed at Mom, who was snoring loudly on the couch, her mouth slightly open. Sinking into a chair, I closed my eyes, wondering what I should do now. If only Glenn or Sonia were here, then maybe I'd know what to do next.

Tía Lola's voice suddenly brightened, "Maybe your *prima*, Antonia, can help. She's your mom's *ahijada*. Well, Antonia got pregnant, dropped out of high school and can't find a job. She told me that if I ever needed help to call her."

I felt the heavy burden lifting as I leaned forward to ask, "You don't think Mom would get mad and try to kick her out?"

"*No sé, hija*, but we can tell María that Antonia doesn't have a place to stay, make her think she's helping out her *ahijada*. She might just let her stay. You know how your mom's always helping everyone out."

Maybe Tía Lola is right, I thought, remembering all the troubled souls Mom had taken in over the years. Robert always used to tease Mom that she was running a boarding house. "It's worth a try," I finally agreed as Tía Lola reached for the telephone.

Antonia came by the next morning and just as we had instructed her, she explained to Mom that her parents had kicked her out of the house. "*Y está esperando un niño*," Tía Lola added.

Although Mom didn't seem to recognize her, she agreed to let Antonia move in for a few days. That same day, I called Robert at work to let him know that I had found another solution and that I would be returning to California. Robert was his usual pessimistic self, "Sonia, you're just avoiding the inevitable."

But I wouldn't let Robert discourage me. "We have to keep Mom at home for as long as possible," I sternly reminded him. "After all, Mom took care of us when we were little. Now it's time to help her."

SEVEN

Rudy

I'm about to dial Juanita's number when Dad calls me into the living room where he's watching the afternoon news. They're showing the most recent bombings in Iraq, and I have to avert my eyes from the TV screen. It seems like every day now, innocent people are killed.

"Rudy," Dad begins, "your mom and I are going to Raquela's wedding this afternoon. We're leaving Amá with you and Manuel."

"But I have plans tonight. Juanita and I are supposed to go out. Can't Manuel watch her?"

Overhearing, Manuel sticks his head into the living room to complain. "I'm not watching her by myself, no way." Then he disappears before I can convince him to change his mind.

"You're the oldest. It's your responsibility," Dad orders, switching the channel to the Bruins basketball game. Heat rushing to my face, I search for Mom in the back patio where she is standing next to Abuela watching her water the different flowers and plants Mom has acquired over the years. "Mom, why do I have to watch her tonight?" I angrily protest.

Abuela seems unaware of my presence as she gently whispers to each plant. Her mouth tightly set, Mom answers, "Sorry, *m'ijo*, you know your dad and I hardly ever go out, but we promised his *compadre*."

"Why can't she stay with Mrs. Garza?" I gripe, but Mom shakes her head.

"Mrs. Garza is going to Los Angeles to visit her sister. Besides, she helps me all week with Amá. She needs a break."

I'm about to say something I know I'll regret when Abuela straightens her bent body and turns around to hand me a ripe cherry tomato. "*Cómetelo, hijo. Es saludable*."

Our eyes meeting, and I halfheartedly take the tomato from her small wrinkled hand, mustering a "Thank you." Now, I don't have the heart to say anything more, and I go back inside to call Juanita, who seems to take the bad news better than me. She even offers to come by to help me babysit Abuela.

Once Mom and Dad have gone, Abuela invites Manuel and me into the kitchen to eat some *caldo* with her. As Abuela hands Manuel a plate of *caldo*, he grumbles, "I'm eating in my room." I remind him that Mom has a rule about eating at the table, but Manuel sneers, "Yeah, well, she's not here." Then he disappears from the kitchen.

I'm about to offer Abuela an explanation for Manuel's punk attitude, but her expressionless face tells me his behavior hasn't fazed her one bit. Out of the corner of my eye, I watch Abuela reach for the salt and begin to sprinkle it on her *caldo*. *There she goes again*, I think to myself, watching her move on to the pepper. But when her hand reaches for the sugar bowl, I grab it away from her, stating, "That's not for *caldo*."

Abuela scowls, reaching for the salt shaker again, but this time I don't stop her. Besides, it's not my problem.

By the time I'm finished with my second bowl of *caldo*, Abuela has forgotten all about the sugar bowl, and she's already at the sink washing dishes. Handing her my plate, I go into the living room to watch TV. I'm completely immersed in the first *Matrix* movie, when Abuela appears at my side carrying a rectangular green box.

"What's that?" I ask as she sits next to me on the couch. Her face brightening, Abuela opens the box and pulls out a picture. "This was your *abuelo*, Rodolfo. You're named after him."

"Oh, yeah?" I say, staring at the dark-skinned man whose plump cheeks and pudgy nose make it crystal clear who I resemble. There is a huge smile on his face, and he's dressed like Antonio Aguilar in his *charro* outfit with his matching boots and leather belt.

Abuela hands me another black-and-white photograph. "Is that you?" I ask, scrutinizing the pretty lady dressed in a simple lace wedding dress. Her black hair is neatly covered by her wedding veil, highlighting her sculpted cheekbones. Now my grandfather is wearing an even cheesier black *charro* outfit with gold tassels. His black sombrero hangs at his side.

"Rodolfo was so handsome. He used to love his sombrero, wore it to all the fiestas."

We are interrupted by a light knocking on the door. "Hey, baby," I greet Juanita at the door.

When I lean forward to kiss her on the lips, Juanita pulls back, gasping, "Rudy! Your *abuelita* might see us!"

"So?" I answer, and as she follows me into the living room, Juanita repeats her warning.

Abuela is still rummaging through her collection of old photographs. "*Buenas noches*, Señora Pérez," Juanita politely greets her.

"You remember my girlfriend Juanita?" I ask, and Abuela nods, handing Juanita a picture.

Smiling, Juanita tells her, "I love to look at pictures. My Amá has this big album of my grandparents, and I never get tired of looking at it."

Abuela continues to take out one picture after another, passing them to Juanita.

"Check this one out," I say, handing Juanita Abuela's wedding day photograph. Then I turn to Abuela and smugly confess, "Me and Juanita are getting married like you and Rodolfo. And we're having five kids!"

Juanita's cheeks turn apple red, and she tells Abuela, "It's a good thing I'm planning on being a teacher, otherwise I don't know how we'd afford all those kids, especially since Rudy doesn't want to go to college."

"That's right, I'm going to get me a good job, make real good money."

Juanita wrinkles her nose as Abuela pulls out another photograph from the box. Pointing to the young girl with the braids standing next to her, Abuela tells me, "*Es Laura, tu mamá.*"

Giggling, Juanita points out Mom's crooked front teeth. Before Abuela can put the picture back in the box, I ask her if I can have it, and she instantly hands it to me. "I think I'll start my own album," I inform Juanita, who seems surprised.

When Manuel suddenly appears in the room, I hold up my grandfather's picture, saying, "This is who I was named after."

Manuel shrugs his shoulders, muttering, "So?" Then he asks if he can go hang out with Jordan, but I remind him that he's supposed to help me all evening. Disgusted, Manuel scoffs, "I'm going upstairs."

After Juanita helps Abuela rearrange her pictures back in the green box, she asks me to switch the channel to *Sábado Gigante*. In her smooth Spanish accent, Juanita explains to Abuela that it's her parents' favorite program, only Abuela's expression is distant, as if she's checked out somewhere far away.

We spend the next hour watching Don Francisco perform some more idiotic stunts with the audience. At times, Abuela attempts a smile, but for the most part, she stares blankly at the TV screen. As the show finally comes to an end, Juanita rises to her feet. "I have to go," she announces. "I told Dad I'd be back by ten."

Explaining to Abuela that I'll only be gone for five minutes, I walk Juanita back to her apartment. But when I return, Abuela is no longer in the living room. Pangs of guilt pounding in my head, I hurry to the kitchen, but she's not there either. Taking the stairs two at a time, I look inside her bedroom, but it's also empty. I fling the door open to my room, hollering at Manuel, who has his stupid earphones on, to get off his ass and help me look for Abuela.

Hurrying back downstairs, I notice the flickers of light coming from the outside patio. I catch a glimpse of Abuela bent over watering her plants. Sighing with relief, I step out into the cool evening air and take her by the arm. "It's really late, Abuela. Let's go inside. You can water your chiles tomorrow."

Her watering can in her hand, Abuela follows me inside. By now, Manuel is standing at the bottom of the stairway. "Is she crazy or what?" he rudely asks.

"Shut up," I answer defensively, wishing Mom and Dad had never left me alone with Abuela.

EIGHT

By the time I wake up on Sunday morning, Manuel's bed is empty. Lately, it seems like Manuel is always gone, but who am I to complain? I get to take as long as I want in the bathroom without having to listen to him bang on the door, insisting my time is up. Sometimes I take my sweet time shaving just to irritate him. Last night, he was no help at all with Abuela. He's damn lucky I didn't tell Mom on him.

As I step into the kitchen, I'm surprised to find Mom by herself. She is sitting at the table with her checkbook in front of her, and it looks as if she's been making out some bills. "Hi, Mom. Where's everyone?" I ask, opening the refrigerator door.

"Your dad's at the dump with his *compadre,* and Abuela stayed with Mrs. Garza and her daughter, visiting from Bakersfield. They were having *menudo* after church. You should've seen how excited Amá got when she saw Mrs. Garza's new baby granddaughter. She wanted to hold her right away."

Sitting across from Mom with my slice of leftover pizza, I say, "That's cool. But I don't know about Abuela holding a baby."

"She was fine. We were all watching her carefully. *Hijo*, thanks for watching Amá last night. It was late when we got home, so we didn't get a chance to talk. Did everything go all right?"

I'm about to complain that Manuel was useless and that I freaked when I couldn't find Amá, but the hopeful look on Mom's face keeps me from telling her the truth. "Yeah, it was fine," I lie, feeling my nose grow like Pinocchio's. "She showed me all the pictures in her album. She even gave me one of you and her when you were a little girl."

Mom gives me a wistful smile. "If you could have seen Amá back then. She was the most beautiful of all your *tías*, that's why your grandfather fell madly in love with her."

"He did?" I ask, thinking that maybe I am a lot like my grandfather since that's exactly how I fell in love with Juanita.

"And how Abuela loved to dance. I remember when we used to go to parties at their *compadres*. She and Apá were the first ones dancing. Amá was also the best cook in the entire family. I must have been around seven when she taught me how to make tortillas." Mom's voice falters, her eyes brimming with tears. "*Pobre* Amá. Now she can't even remember how to do anything."

"She gave Manuel and me some *caldo* last night," I offer, hoping to soothe Mom's hurt.

"That's good," Mom whispers, wiping away a tear and reaching for the letter opener. She lets out a heavy sigh when she reads the water bill. "I can't believe it. They raised the water again."

"I get paid next week if you need some money."

"Thanks, *m'ijo*. But you need it for your own expenses. Gas is so expensive now. Anyway, your dad said they were gonna give him some overtime this month."

I'm not easily fooled by Mom's explanation. "Okay, but if you change your mind, let me know," I tell her, rising from the table,

In the living room, I dial Juanita's number. It rings and rings. Hanging up, I remember that last night she told me she was going with her family to a *quinceañera* in San Martín. When I asked if I was invited, Juanita had shrugged, '"Don't push your luck with my dad, Rudy."' Now I wish I *had* pushed it, then I'd be with Juanita instead of here all alone.

I decide to borrow Mom's car to see if Tyrone wants to hang out, only when I get to his apartment, he's busy washing his car. "It's a miracle you're not with Juanita," he grins up at me.

"Look who's talking. Why don't you take your car to the car wash? It'd be a lot easier."

Shaking his head, Tyrone admits, "I'm not lazy like you. I enjoy washing it myself."

"What's Maya up to today?"

Tyrone pauses to wipe the sweat from his brow. "She's waiting for me to pick her up so we can go to the beach. And Juanita?"

"She's with her family today, but, man, I sure wish she were here."

Tyrone fixes his gaze on me. "Oh, yeah? What's up? You seem kind of down."

"It's my grandma. She's driving everyone in my family nuts, and Mom's been worried about her health. Then money's tight with an extra person in the house."

"Yeah, it's hard. When my dad left us, I thought Mom was gonna have a nervous breakdown with all the bills. That's why I got a job so I could help her out. But now everything's better."

"I'm really glad school is almost out. I'll be working full-time then, so I can really help Mom."

"Don't you remember what we learned in Consumer Math?" Tyrone asks sarcastically. "Minimum wage, Rudy. That doesn't go very far. "

"I better go. You're beginning to sound like my counselor."

"I wish Juanita would knock some sense into you," Tyrone calls out as I head back to my car.

The hours seem to drag by. Wondering what time Juanita is getting home, I cruise around downtown for a while, but all I see are tourists or couples walking hand in hand. I end up feeling even more alone, so I head back to the apartment. When I get there, Mom and Abuela are in the living room. Abuela has taken all of the photographs out of the green box and is messing with them while Mom watches the cooking channel. For once, I don't mind the sissy-looking chef since Mom sounds relaxed when she greets me, her gaze fixed on the screen.

When Abuela calls out for me to look at her wedding photograph as if I've never seen it before, I want to tell her I've already seen it, but I don't. Mumbling that I have homework, I exit the room, wishing I could talk with Juanita instead of some crazy old lady.

Upstairs in my room, I kick my feet up on the bed and try to chill out with some old issues of *Muscle Up*. Then I put on one of my Los Lonely Boys CDs. Hours later, when Juanita finally calls, I reluctantly confess that I had a miserable day without her. "*Pobrecito*," she says, going on to describe the *quinceañera* in detail. I don't get any sympathy until I tell her about my conversation with Mom.

"Sometimes moms won't talk about what's bothering them because they don't want their kids to worry," she says.

"Maybe Manuel was right. Maybe it was a mistake for my grandma to come live with us. Ever since she got here, everything's all screwed up."

"*Ay*, Rudy, don't be so insensitive."

"What do you mean 'insensitive'? We guys are sweet and sensitive."

Giggling loudly into the phone, Juanita teases me back. "Wait until I tell Maya what you just said."

"Yeah, well she oughta know. She's got her own Macho Man."

When Juanita starts to giggle again, I imagine her two giant dimples and all of a sudden, I want to cover her sweet face with kisses.

NINE

It's the final week of school before Christmas break and everyone is jazzed up. Some of the girls are wearing Santa hats or jingle bells on their shoes. It's really sick the way Mr. Marshall, the principal, walks around with the stupidest looking Rudolph the Reindeer tie. It's wide at the top and it has a big red nose that makes a honking sound. Mr. Marshall goes around honking at all the students. And some of the classrooms that participated in the door decorating contest have the wildest holiday scenes on their doors with everything from hip-hop elves to red and green Shaq sleigh shoes.

On Wednesday in my Consumer Math class, holiday shopping becomes a central focus as Mrs. Montrose discusses the pitfalls of credit cards and how people abuse them at Christmastime. Ronnie, one of the Barbie girls from the country club, raises her hand to say, "But it's cool getting all those presents. How are we supposed to get them without credit cards?"

Someone lets out a loud groan, and Jackie says, "People are spoiled in this country."

"Yeah, that's right, Jackie," I speak up. "In some countries, people don't even get enough food to eat."

Ronnie gives me a cold stare, and before I can express what I really think about her snobby attitude, Mrs. Montrose begins to discuss the special Christmas accounts offered by banks which allow people to deduct money automatically from their paychecks all year long. "These accounts provide an effective alternative to the overuse of credit cards during the holidays."

"I think people should just stop buying so much stuff," Jackie states, glancing with disdain at Ronnie.

"Frankly, I agree with you," Mrs. Montrose says, "but the reality is that we live in a consumer-oriented society." As the bell rings for the end of third period, I think of Manuel and all the stuff he's constantly asking Mom and Dad to buy for him even though he doesn't need it. Then I think of all the stuff advertised on the TV commercials. It's no wonder we're always consuming instead of saving.

Juanita, Maya, and Rina are waiting for me next to my locker. "Hey," I smile, pulling Juanita to my side as I dial the combination on my locker. Then I turn to Maya and ask for Tyrone and like always, big-mouth Rina answers. "He's helping with the Senior Food Drive. *Apúrate*—we're eating at Hound Dogs today."

"I hate wiener dogs!" I complain, slamming my locker shut.

Bemused, Juanita smiles sweetly while Rina shouts, "That's cause you're a little weenie!"

I give her a slight jab on the shoulder before we head down the hallway.

"Can't you two ever get along?" Maya asks, exchanging an exasperated look with Juanita.

A short while later, we pull into Hound Dogs, only today, we go inside since there is a long wait at the drive-up window. We get in line behind some little old lady whose wrinkled skin and thin gray hair remind me of Abuela. While we wait, Rina brings up Christmas. "Hey, *mosco*, what are you getting Juanita for Christmas?"

"None of your business," I answer, ignoring Rina's glare. The truth is, I hate shopping and Juanita knows it.

While Maya cheerfully begins to describe the leather jacket she has on layaway for Tyrone, I can't help but notice how rude and impatient the knob-nosed guy at the counter is acting toward the lady in front of us. Raising his voice, Knob Nose sarcastically repeats the amount she owes for her order. The lady, who is struggling with the zipper on her purse, appears more flustered, and her hands start to shake even more. The rude waiter begins to impatiently tap his fingers on the counter.

"Ma'am, can I open that for you?" I offer to help.

"Would you please?" she whispers, catching my gaze. I reach over and unzip her purse, making sure I cast a mean look at Knob Nose, who hasn't taken his eyes off of us. Thanking me, the lady takes out several neatly folded dollar bills from her purse and hands them to Knob Nose, who mutters something under his breath. Then, reaching for her food, she thanks me again before she turns toward the entrance.

By now, the conversation about Christmas presents has come to an end. "That was nice of you," Juanita says, squeezing my arm while Maya smiles in agreement.

"Yeah, I didn't know you had it in you!" Rina quips as Knob Nose asks for our order.

Once we're seated at a booth eating our wiener dogs, Juanita asks Maya about her Mom's trip to New Mexico. Maya sighs, "I guess Grandma's a lot worse now, but Mom couldn't bear placing her in a home, so she found a cousin who's going to take care of her."

"That's good," Juanita says.

"I don't know what my mom would do if Abuela got that sick—she'd go nuts," Rina admits.

Maya smiles uncomfortably. "Mom's totally depressed about Grandma getting Alzheimer's. She snaps at me for any little thing these days."

"Is that what happens with Alzheimer's?" I ask, thinking about Mom and how depressed she seems.

"I told you to come talk to my mom about it," Maya says, but I shrug my shoulders, pretending everything's cool. Only I know it isn't.

The tardy bell rings as Rina and I rush to our seats in Spanish class. Sr. Villamil, who is taking attendance, glances at us and in his weird Puerto Rican accent, he announces, "*Ya llegaron los reyes de Roma*."

"Yeah, I'm the king all right," I answer in Spanish, and the room fills with chuckles when Rina says that I'm *el rey de los pedos*. If anyone is a fart, it's her.

We spend the entire period wrapping presents for the children at the Women's Haven. It was Rina's idea. For once, she actually made some sense. She told Mr. Villamil about all the kids at the women's shelter whose mothers can't afford to buy them presents for Christmastime. Then she came up with the idea of having the Spanish Club sell *pan dulce* during the games. Rina's idea was great.

After fifth period, I catch the bus to Discount Foods, where I spend the afternoon going from one station to the next bagging groceries. Since we're short-handed at the counters, the manager gives me permission to skip the floor sweep. When Myrna calls me to her station to bag groceries for one of her customers, I recognize the sandy-haired woman whose father was lost in the store a few weeks ago. Pushing her grocery cart outside, I ask about her father. "We had to put him in a home," she answers with twinges of disappointment in her voice.

Embarrassed, I offer an apology, as she opens the door to her minivan.

When I get home that evening, Mom and Manuel are having a heated conversation in the living room. Manuel is begging Mom for an iPod for Christmas, but Mom tells him, "*Hijo*, we can't afford it this year."

Refusing to accept Mom's explanation, Manuel bristles, "It's because of her, isn't it? That's why we're so broke."

Mom tries to reason with Manuel, but he heads for the stairs, yelling out, "I wish she'd go back where she came from!"

Noticing the tears in Mom's eyes, I mutter under my breath, "That little punk."

TEN

Friday afternoon is like a circus with students rushing through hallways, eager for the holiday break. The parking lot is even noisier with groups of students hurrying to their cars, then weaving their way amidst the orange school buses. Gathered around Maya's car, she cheerfully suggests, "Why don't we grab some burgers and go out to the beach?"

"Sorry, babe," Tyrone apologizes. "I promised Ray I'd help out at the Teen Center today—he's doing something on Kwanzaa."

"How cool," Maya answers, repeating her suggestion about going to the beach.

Waving to Tyrone, we continue with our beach plans. When Tommy suggests we all go in his dad's car, I roll my eyes, saying, "Yeah, but you know Rina won't fit. We need two cars for her."

Rina smacks me on the shoulder, and I pretend to wince in pain while Sheena warns, "Better watch out, Rudy—Rina's been pumping weights."

"Oh, I'm so scared," I say, shaking my hands in the air.

Laughing, Ankiza explains that she can't go with us. "I told Mom I'd babysit Athena while she goes shopping."

"I can't go either," Sheena sighs. "I signed up for the afternoon shift at McDonalds. As much as I hate that place, I'm trying to save up my money so I can get my own place this summer. Sorry."

"I'm sure glad I don't have to work this afternoon," Rina admits.

"Too bad!" I instantly reply, and Rina tries to smack me again, but I dodge her blow by moving behind Juanita.

"Come on, let's go. I'll drop you off at work," Ankiza tells Sheena, who warns me again about Rina's muscles as they turn to leave.

Maya is insistent that we take her car, but before we get on the freeway, we make a quick stop at McDonalds for burgers and sodas. Then we take the scenic ten-minute drive to Tomol Beach, which has become the number one spot for evening bonfires or graduation parties on the beach. On weekends, Tomol Beach is also flooded with tourists and university students who come to sunbathe or cruise the waters in their sailboats or kayaks. I once asked my Social Studies teacher what the word *Tomol* means and he said it is a Chumash word that means canoe. Then he pointed out the entire Central Coast once belonged to the Chumash people whose indigenous culture flourished here for over thousands of years. You'd never know it from all the fancy tourist resorts and million-dollar homes that have popped up in the area.

Today, there aren't too many people at Tomol Beach. We park several blocks away from the waterfront, but we don't mind the short walk since it's a warm December day. There is a light breeze, and the blue-gray sky is dotted with seagulls. Tomol Beach lies in a crescent with huge granite cliffs that stretch along the coastline. It has three piers that stretch out above the sapphire blue waves. The longest pier is situated on the other side of the crescent, and it holds several exclusive seafood restaurants. There is a smaller pier in the middle, which is closed to the public. The third pier is the busiest since it is directly across from Main Street, and it holds a variety of California beachfront shops and restaurants. I once went inside one of these shops with Maya and Juanita, and I couldn't believe the outrageous prices they charged for the silliest things like seashell can openers. But I guess tourists have a lot of money to spend.

When we get to the waterfront, we take off our shoes, picking a comfortable spot where we have a nice view of the ocean and the entire coastline. While we eat our burgers and fries, the conversation centers on graduation.

"We oughta have our senior party here, a mega bonfire," Rina suggests.

"That's exactly what we're planning," Maya says, thrusting a handful of fries in her mouth.

"It's gonna be sad moving away from here," Tommy admits, his hazel eyes brighter now from the sunlight.

"Don't worry," Maya comments. "We'll see each other on breaks. Besides, San Francisco State is near Stanford."

"Yeah, but it won't be the same," Tommy sighs.

Then Juanita turns to Rina, "Have you decided what you're going to do?"

"Yeah, Rina, make us happy . . . tell us you're going far away," I reply, grinning.

"Shut up," Rina says, flinging a french fry at me. Then she looks at Juanita, sighing, "I'm not sure. I know I have to keep working to help Mom out, but Mr. Villamil has been talking to me about taking classes at the local college."

"*¡Qué suave!*" Juanita exclaims. "Then you can transfer to Laguna University and take classes with me and Tyrone. Wish I could talk Rudy into doing that too."

Now everyone's eyes are on me, but I refuse to feel like a loser. "That school stuff isn't for me," I tritely answer. "I'm planning on getting a good job, make some money." Then, hoping to avoid another lecture on why I should go to college, I grab Juanita by the hand. "Come on, let's play Frisbee."

Soon we're all tossing the Frisbee around. When it lands in the water and starts to float away, I double-dare Rina to go after it. Refusing to back down from my dare, Rina trudges into the waves after the Frisbee. Seconds later, she emerges victorious while Maya and Juanita begin to cheer loudly, "Xicana power! Latina power!"

Her jeans soaked, Rina triumphantly, takes a bow as if she were the new female president of Chile. By now, the ocean breeze has picked up, and it's starting to cool off, so we decide to gather up our stuff and return to the car.

Shutting the front door behind me, I hear a Spanish commercial blaring from the TV, but when I walk into the living room, no one is there. Just as I am about to head upstairs, Abuela opens the outside patio door, calling out, "*Rodolfo, ven acá.*" Abuela is dressed weirdly today. She's wearing a long-sleeved shirt under a short-sleeved summer dress, and it's buttoned wrong.

"Aren't you cold, Abuela?" I ask, following her to the patio. Ignoring my question, she leads me to a crate where she has planted some herbs.

"This is *hierbabuena*," she explains. Then she points to the next plant saying, "And this is *manzanilla*."

"Oh, yeah?" I reply, noticing the muddy soil from all the water she's added.

"*Manzanilla* is good for stomach aches. Once your mom got sick, barely two months old, we thought she was gonna die, she kept throwing up. But I gave her *té de manzanilla* all night until she finally got better. And this is anise. Your *abuelo* told me the Indians used it to cure *reumas*. *Huélelo*," she says, pinching off a leaf so that I can smell it.

"It smells like licorice," I tell her, and she nods quietly.

Abuela is about to point out another herb when the door flings open and an irate Manuel appears in the patio. Holding up some empty CD cases, he shouts, "Abuela, did you take the CDs that were in here?" Manuel's cheeks are flushed, and there is a bitterness in his voice.

Abuela meekly shakes her head, but Manuel continues to accuse her. "Don't lie, Abuela. I found these in your room. Where are my CDs?" Now Abuela looks rattled, and her hands tremble slightly as she moves away toward her herbs. Only Manuel raises his voice even more. "I know you took them. Give them back!"

Abuela suddenly bursts into tears, and it takes all of my self-control to keep from slugging Manuel. "Get out of here!" I grumble, giving him a slight push until he finally retreats through the open door. I place my arm around Abuela's thin shoulder, advising her not to pay attention to Manuel because he's just a spoiled little punk who doesn't know what he's talking about. "Abuela, how about we go out front to look for some rocks?" I ask, thinking this might help. "I saw some real shiny ones by the mailboxes."

Her face brightening, Abuela's tears subside as I take her by the hand through the apartment and out front where we begin to search for rocks. Once our pockets are full, I help Abuela carry her new collection of rocks upstairs to her bedroom where she places them in an empty glass bowl at her bedside. There are rocks neatly placed on top of her dresser, on her nightstand, and in every possible space. "Here, *hijo*—this one's for you," she smiles, handing me a small rock from her Virgen de Guadalupe jewelry box.

"Thanks, Abuela," I answer, placing it in my pocket.

Rushing into my bedroom, I walk up to Manuel, who is busy rearranging his CDs on his dresser. I grab him firmly by the collar. "Don't ever disrespect Abuela like that again, you hear me?" I say threateningly. "She's sick, and you know it."

"Okay, okay, lay off of me," Manuel begs as I reluctantly release him, wishing I could give him a beating he'll never forget.

ELEVEN

Professor Sonia Gonzales

The call came in the middle of the night. Robert was hysterical. Mom had disappeared on Saturday while Antonia was taking a shower. Tía Luisa had notified everyone, and they'd searched in the neighborhood for Mom, but when it started to get late and they still couldn't find her, they'd notified the police. Late that evening, someone reported they'd seen an elderly woman dressed in her nightgown wandering on Anaya Boulevard. According to Robert, they'd had to restrain Mom in order to get her in the police car. "It's time, Sonia," Robert tersely stated. "No one can take care of her anymore."

The next morning, I explained to Maya that I would have to go back to Santa Fe. "Maybe you can spend Christmas in the Bay area with your dad," I suggested, not wanting to ruin the holidays for Maya.

"Mom, do you think I'd spend Christmas without you? I'm going with you."

I'd burst into tears, and Maya had put her arms around me then, saying, "Don't cry, Mom. You watch—everything will work out."

"But what about your birthday?" I asked, "You were planning on having a party here with your friends."

Maya's perfect brown eyes widened. "I can celebrate it in New Mexico like I did before. Don't you remember? It was awesome being with my cousins on my birthday."

"Yes, *mi'ja*," I remember," I agreed, thinking back to how much Mom had loved birthdays. That December, she had bought Maya a huge colorful Mickey Mouse piñata and made tamales for her. Only now, things would be entirely different.

On Sunday, Glenn drove us to the airport. As we kissed goodbye, he promised to call from Sacramento where he would be spending Christmas with his parents. During the flight, I listened absentmindedly while Maya chatted about spring break and driving to Tijuana with her friends. At one point, Maya paused to stroke my hand, saying, "Don't worry, Mom. We'll be there soon."

When we de-planed in Albuquerque, Jesse, Tío Jesus' oldest son, was waiting for us as at the baggage claim area. Jesse, who was in his third year at the University of New Mexico, had always been one of Mom's favorite nephews. "Hey, Jess," Maya greeted him as they hugged.

"You've gotten taller," I told Jesse as he returned my hug.

On the one-hour drive to Mom's house, Jesse answered Maya's questions about UNM, occasionally chuckling at her naiveté about dorm life. Yet all I could do was think about Mom and the decision that lay ahead for me. How am I going to survive all of this? I asked myself, staring blankly at the panoramic views of Northern New Mexico.

Tía Lola was sitting in Dad's faded armchair when we arrived. I glanced at Mom, who was asleep on the couch. *Probably from all the tranquilizers*, I thought as Tía Lola rose to her feet. "I'm glad you're here, *hija*," she said. "Antonia just left." Moving closer to embrace Maya, she added, "You've grown taller, *mi'jita. Pero todavía eres una flaquita como tu mamá.*"

Giggling, Maya replied, "And you've shrunk, Tía!" We all smiled, even Jesse, who was returning with the luggage. Borrowing my cell phone so that she could call Tyrone, Maya disappeared into one of the bedrooms.

After Jesse left, I turned to Tía Lola, asking, "Is Mom any better?

Tía Lola shook her head sadly. "No, *hija.* She's only quiet when we give her the pills. Antonia had to call Dr. Lewis for a stronger dosage. He agreed, but he said it's time to make some arrangements—that we can't continue to drug her up like that. I told him you were on your way."

I couldn't speak for a moment, losing myself in Mom's rhythmic snores, staring intently at the face of the woman I'd loved most in my life, the woman who had given me life, who had taught me all of my values. The ringing of the telephone interrupted my thoughts.

Tía Lola handed me the receiver. "It's Roberto."

I felt the knots tightening in my chest as I said hello to Robert. "How's Maya?" he right away asked.

"She's fine—happy to be here. What time are you coming by tomorrow?"

"That's why I called. I have to work."

Raising my voice, I demanded, "But, Robert, I *need* your help."

"I told you, Sonia, I can't. I have to work. Now it's your time to handle it. You've always had it so easy being far away."

"How dare you!" I cried, slamming the receiver down unwilling to accept any more of his accusations.

"*¿Qué pasó, hija?*" Tía Lola carefully asked.

"Robert refuses to come help me."

Shaking her head, Tía Lola repeated a few comforting words as I stared at my drugged up mother lying helplessly on the couch like a discarded object.

After Tía Lola left, I covered Mom with a blanket, relieved that she would sleep through the night. Attempting to cheer me up, Maya reappeared, suggesting we watch a movie. "*The Wedding Singer* is on—you love that movie!"

Smiling, I sunk into Dad's comfortable recliner as Adam Sandler came on the screen singing with his silly guitar. Within seconds, I was relaxed and giggling with Maya like a teenager.

Early the next morning, I awoke to find Mom frantically packing up all her knickknacks in paper bags. She had already taken most of the family pictures off the walls and they lay at her side wrapped in towels or dishcloths. When I saw her reach for the telephone and disconnect it, I cried out, "Mom, what are you doing?"

"I have to go home," she replied angrily as I snatched the telephone from her, plugging it back into the wall.

"You're already home," I replied, but Mom only shook her head, removing more knickknacks from the entertainment set. Hurrying to retrieve her pills from my suitcase, I returned with a glass of water and although she resisted, I waited until she had swallowed each one of them.

By the time Maya awakened, the pills began to take effect, and Mom was calm. Within a half hour, she was completely knocked out on the couch. Drawing in a long breath, I turned to Maya and said, "Sorry, *mi'ja*, there's nothing edible. Mom made a mess in the refrigerator. Why don't you go over to Tía Lola's for breakfast? Come to think of, it might be best if you stayed there. Besides, your birthday is the day after tomorrow—it's impossible to do anything here."

Maya wrinkled her nose. "Okay, Mom. But don't worry about my birthday—I know Grandma's sick."

By the following day, I had convinced Maya to stay with her cousins. Relieved that she was gone, I spent the next few days like a prisoner confined to her cell. I had to keep all of my possessions locked in my suitcase since Mom constantly wandered in and out of the bedrooms, moving things around and hiding them in the strangest places. I was even forced into hiding essentials like toilet paper and coffee under my bed. The doctor had warned me that Mom would build resistance to the pills, so I wasn't surprised that it was taking longer for her to get drowsy. Only now, she had taken to wandering off in the middle of the day. Several times, I'd had to call one of Tío Jesus' sons to help me find her and bring her home. The pounding in my chest was increasing and my cell phone seemed to be my only companion.

When Maya came by with her cousin Nicole, I did my best to mask my depression. "Happy birthday, *m'ija*. How does it feel to be seventeen?"

Her usual jubilant self, Maya answered, "Awesome, and wait till you see the cake Tía Lola baked me . . . it's shaped like a New Mexican chile!"

Nicole, who had always been one of my favorite nieces, politely asked if I would like to join them for a movie. Thanking her, I turned to Maya and said, "Sorry, *mi'ja*. I can't leave Mom alone. But go and have some fun with your cousins."

Later that day, when Tía Lola came by to check on Mom, I broke down in front of her. Tía Lola embraced me, saying, "Sonia, *hija*, you have to make the decision today. Just look at you! You're pale, thin. You can't take care of her by yourself. Why don't you go and make the call right now?"

"I hate to do it," I whispered, glancing at Mom, who was snoring peacefully on the couch.

Tía Lola squeezed my hand. "*No te preocupes, hija.* María doesn't know anything anymore. And you have to do it before she hurts herself or gets run over by a car."

Tears burning my eyes, I went into the bedroom and made the call to Jan Miller, Director of the Sage Nursing Home. She was sympathetic and kind, agreeing to make all the necessary arrangements for Mom's admission.

On Christmas Eve, we drove Mom to the Sage Nursing Home. I was thankful that Maya came along. I was feeling terrified about Mom's reaction. But I had followed Jan's instructions and given Mom pills earlier than usual so that she would be less agitated. Tía Lola was in the backseat with Mom, who kept on repeating in Spanish, "*Ya me voy a la casa*."

When we pulled into the parking lot at the nursing home, Mom refused to get out of the car, but I explained that she was home. "*Ésta es tu casa,* María," Tía Lola repeated to her, so Mom meekly nodded, finally sliding out of the backseat.

Jan met us at the entrance with Barb, the kind nurse who had answered all of my questions on that first visit. We exchanged a few brief words. Noticing that Mom was getting agitated again, I quickly led her into the building, following Jan and Barb toward the Alzheimer's unit. When Jan pushed the red button to open the door, Mom seemed frightened. Her fear increased as we proceeded through the TV room and made our way down the hallway to the small room that would serve as Mom's new home. Turning to face Mom, Barb gently explained, "María, this is your bed."

The last thing I would remember was the look of terror on Mom's face as I fled from the room, leaving her behind with Maya and Tía Lola. Outside, I burst into tears, paralyzed with grief from the knowledge of what I'd just done to my own mother.

TWELVE

Professor Sonia Gonzales

As soon as we returned to Mom's house, I went into the bedroom and flung myself on her bed, sobbing until my eyes felt swollen. After that, I lay still, staring at Mom's dressing table—her favorite perfumes, the heart-shaped jewelry box Dad had given her one Christmas, the small photo of Maya and me on the mirror along with those of her godchildren, nieces, and nephews. My eyes wandered to all the stuff Mom had crammed into her bedroom this past year from garden tools to kitchen utensils. The thought of Mom sleeping amidst the cobwebs and dust-filled clutter brought another flurry of tears to my eyes. How will I go on with my life now? I thought, feeling depressed and lonely.

Just then, there was a light tap on the door, and Maya entered carrying a cup of tea. "Mom, are you feeling better? *Híjole,* Grandma's room is trashed."

Leaning up against the headboard, I took the cup of tea from her. "I'm better, thanks, *m'ija*. And Tía Lola?"

"She had to leave, but she wants us to go by her house tonight."

We were interrupted by the sound of the telephone, and Maya hurried to answer it. I could hear her talking in a hushed voice while I sipped my tea. After a few minutes, Maya reappeared, saying, "Mom, it's for you—it's Glenn."

I slowly lifted myself off the bed and went into the living room. "Sonia, are you okay?" Glenn asked. "I tried your cell phone earlier, but it must've been turned off. Maya told me you took your Mom today."

I tried to speak, but my voice broke. Glenn waited a moment, then he gently said, "I know this decision must be tearing you apart, but sweetheart, you did the right thing. There's no way you or anyone else could've taken care of her—even Robert."

"I guess so," I hesitated, "But one day Robert will regret his selfishness."

"Yes, I'm sure he will. I only wish I could be there to help you get through this."

"Me too," I whispered, wishing Glenn weren't thousands of miles away. "But I'm glad you called. I needed to hear your voice."

We talked for a while longer about Glenn's parents, their tradition of going to midnight mass and the holiday brunch with the entire family. By the time we hung up, the heaviness in my heart felt lighter. Splashing some water on my swollen eyelids, I joined Maya in the living room. She was engrossed in a Christmas special with an unusual cast of stars that included Usher, Los Lonely Boys, and the Dixie Chicks.

"Can we go to Tía Lola's?" Maya asked, glancing at me.

"I'm sorry, Maya. I don't feel like being around anyone tonight. But you go ahead."

Maya frowned, twirling a strand of her long hair round and round. "I can't leave you alone on Christmas Eve. Please, Mom. Tía Lola said she's making tamales for us."

How Mom had loved the family ritual of making tamales. Every Christmas season, she and Tía Lola would spend an entire week on their tamale production—preparing the *masa* until it was perfect, then grinding the chiles for the red sauce. No powdered chile for them! They would recruit everyone from small children to adults to help spread the *masa* on the corn husks. One year, Mom bragged that they'd made thirty dozen tamales, parceling them out to the relatives by Christmas day.

"All right, I'll go for a little while," I reluctantly agreed, knowing Mom would have wanted me to do this.

At Tía Lola's that evening, no one mentioned my puffy eyes, and although the tamales were delicious, it didn't feel the same without Mom there to celebrate with us. When Maya exclaimed, "These are almost as good as Grandma's," Tía Lola sadly confessed that it was her mother's recipe.

"Your *bisabuela* taught María and me how to make them," she proudly told Maya.

Later, as I watched Maya and her cousins gather around the tree to sing Christmas carols, I fought back the tears, remembering how Mom would always join in loudly when they sang "Feliz Navidad." When the time arrived to open presents and Tía Lola whispered, "María always loved opening her presents," I couldn't take it any longer. Bursting into tears, I fled from the room while they looked on with pity.

Robert called the next morning, but I refused to speak with him. "Tell him I'm busy," I ordered Maya, knowing that if I spoke with Robert, I'd only lash out at him.

Although Jan had advised me to wait a few days before I visited Mom, I knew I couldn't leave her alone on Christmas day. At noon, Maya and I drove to the Sage Nursing Home where we found Mom in the dining room seated at a table with two other women. As soon as I called out to her, Mom was on her feet, saying, "*Ya quiero irme a mi casa. Ya vámonos.*"

Trying to ignore Mom's request, I hugged her while Maya promptly took her by the hand, saying, "Let's go see your room, Grandma."

"I want to go home," Mom repeated this time in English as we led her toward the putrid smelling hallway to her room. I recognized the shriveled up woman in the wheelchair heading in our direction. She seemed to be carrying on a conversation with herself. We moved to the other side to let her pass and as she went by, Mom said, "I have to keep the door closed so that crazy *vieja* won't steal my things."

Entering her room, Maya asked, "Grandma, what happened to the pictures we put up on the wall yesterday?"

"They stole them," Mom exclaimed. "Can you take me home now?"

I bit into the inside of my lower lip until I tasted blood.

"Grandma, this is a nice room. You can look out the window at the trees," Maya nervously said.

Only Mom was becoming more anxious, pacing around the small room. "*Quiero irme a mi casa,*" she repeated.

Exchanging a nervous glance with Maya, I asked her to turn on the television to the Spanish station. Then I took a seat on the small bed, holding up the bag of treats I had brought, saying, "Look, Mom, I brought you some pistachios and your favorite—a Snickers bar."

Mom quickly grabbed them from me. "*Qué bueno*— but I have to hide them or they'll take them." Then she walked to the two-drawer chest next to the TV and stuffed them inside a drawer where I spotted one of the framed pictures Maya had asked about. Moving back to my side, Mom asked, "Can we go now?"

"Look, Grandma, it's the Snake Man," Maya said, pointing to the TV screen. With a brief glance, Mom repeated her request, raising her voice slightly.

My hands shaking, I wondered what I should do next. Reaching my purse, I pulled out my wallet and began to show Mom the pictures I carried inside. Now I had her attention. When Mom saw the small photo of my maternal grandmother that she had given me years back, she said, "Mamá Francisca."

"Good thinking," Maya whispered as Mom sat next to me, focusing her attention on the photograph.

After a very long minute, I turned to the next picture of Mom and Dad's twenty-fifth wedding anniversary. "Do you recognize this one?" I asked, trying to sound cheerful.

Mom stared blankly at the photograph until I finally explained, "That's you and Dad—Roberto, your husband." But the blankness remained on her face as I went through several more family pictures. Soon Maya joined in, pointing out how cute she looked in her first-grade picture. Only Mom remained silent. I continued to show her the photographs in my wallet and at times, it seemed as if a spark of memory appeared on her face, but I was left to identify the people in the photographs.

We sat there reviewing the same photographs over and over until Mom suddenly rose to her feet, demanding, "*Ya quiero irme a la casa.*"

Now I understood why Jan had insisted a wait a few days before coming to visit. Steadying my voice, I said, "Mom, you have to stay here now."

When Mom reached for her coat, I glanced at Maya nervously, knowing I needed to think of something quickly. "How about some ice cream?" I suggested, remembering how this had been one of Mom's favorite treats.

Mom's eyes brightened as I grabbed my purse and directed Maya out to the hallway. As we walked back to the reception area, I instructed Maya to be prepared for a quick exit. When I asked the nurse's aide if they had any ice cream, she smiled, "Of course, we do." Then she turned to Mom, saying, "Would you like some ice cream, María?" I was relieved when Mom eagerly nodded.

We went to the TV room to wait, taking a seat across from another female patient who was busy talking to the characters in the soap opera she was watching. I caught Maya's nervous glance as the aide reappeared. "Here you are, María," she said, handing Mom a cup of strawberry ice cream.

While Mom concentrated on eating her ice cream, I gave her a quick kiss, whispering goodbye. Then Maya and I hurried to the entrance, my eyes watering as Maya punched in the code that would open the locked door. Walking away from the Alzheimer's unit, Maya embraced me, saying, "Don't cry, Mom. Grandma will be fine."

Later that afternoon when Tía Marcela called to ask about visiting hours, I angrily chastised her. "You never visited Mom before. Why bother now?" Slamming the phone down, I felt vindicated that someone had finally voiced the truth to Mom's selfish brothers and sisters.

THIRTEEN

Rudy

Christmas Eve is one of the busiest days of the year at Discount Foods. We sell tons of liquor and a lot of hams and turkeys on this day. One man buys seven bottles of wine and as I bag them up for him, he explains that his relatives are coming from Sacramento to visit for the weekend. A tall lady in an expensive-looking suit buys a large bottle of brandy, explaining that every Christmas and New Year's, she makes eggnog for the entire family. Not at my house, I think to myself. We always have Mexican chocolate and *pan dulce* after we eat Mom's mouth-watering tamales.

By three o'clock, the store is packed with customers trying to get home as quickly as possible to their families. The manager instructs us to ignore the afternoon store sweeps and to concentrate on the long lines of impatient customers at the register. I float from one station to the next bagging groceries without any breaks, and by the time my shift ends, my feet are sore.

As I step into the apartment, I'm startled by the unexpected silence. The living room is empty, so I make my way into the kitchen where I find stacks of tamales on the counter waiting to be steamed. I hear the front door opening, and when I turn around, Mom appears at my side. There is a tense expression on her face, and the lines on her forehead are deeper. "*M'ijo*, I can't find Amá. I looked all around the neighborhood, but I can't find her."

"Maybe she's with Manuel."

"No, he's upstairs in his room. He said he hasn't seen her. And it's starting to rain. I don't know what to do," Mom admits, running her hand through her short permed hair.

"Is Dad home yet?"

"He's driving around to see if he can find her. I don't know what happened. I was steaming tamales, and she said she was going to the bathroom. When she didn't come down right away, I got worried. That's when I discovered she was gone."

Now Mom begins to sniffle, so I place my hand on her shoulder. "Don't worry, Mom," I say reassuringly. "We'll find her."

Manuel suddenly appears at the top of the stairs and I'm about to order him to get his lazy butt downstairs to help us when Dad comes rushing into the apartment. He's wearing his tan Laguna Garbage shirt and khaki work pants. Sounding frantic, he explains, "I drove up and down the neighborhood streets, but Dolores is nowhere. I'm going to call the police."

Mom's face turns ashen, as if she is about to faint. I tell her to sit down, but she refuses, following Dad to the telephone. We listen anxiously while Dad speaks with an officer, pausing for a moment to ask Mom about the exact description of the clothes Abuela was wearing today. Hanging up, Dad states wearily, "They want us to file a report in person at the police station."

Nodding in agreement, Mom says, "*Hijo*, you wait here with Manuel in case Amá comes home."

"I will, but don't worry, Mom. We'll find her."

They are about to go out the door when the phone rings. The unfamiliar voice on the other end of the line asks for Dad, so I hand him the receiver. "Yes, that's her. We're on our way," Dad says, hanging up the phone. Then he turns Mom. "Dolores is at the police station. I guess this lady saw her wandering around downtown. When she asked her if she needed some help, Dolores started to cry, so the lady was kind enough to drive her to the police station."

"*Bendito sea Dios*," Mom whispers, tears in her eyes.

Just then, Manuel walks into the room. "Did they find her?" he asks, sounding genuinely concerned about Abuela.

"Yeah, but no thanks to you," I answer sharply.

"Shut up," Manuel says as Dad hurries out the door after Mom.

An hour later, Mom and Dad return with Abuela, who seems unaware of the horrible ordeal she has put us through. "*Rodolfo, estás tan grande*," she exclaims as if she hasn't seen me in years. Returning Abuela's hug, I'm relieved nothing bad happened to her, that she's safely home. Even self-centered Manuel lets Abuela give him a hug before he goes back upstairs.

That evening at dinner, we celebrate with Mom's tamales, which seem to taste even better than last Christmas. Once Mom told me that she learned how to make tamales from Abuela, who learned from her own mother when she was a young girl. I guess that explains why Mom is such a fanatic about the *masa* being perfect. Every year she and Dad drive to San Martín to purchase it from her favorite Mexican store, La Campesina. Mom says they're the only ones who prepare the *masa* the right way. I don't know how she does it, but Mom always makes tons of tamales and then she gives them away to her friends. Mom says that's the best part—sharing them with others.

Tonight Abuela is quieter than usual, but I suppose she's exhausted from all the walking she did today. When Mom asks her a question, she simply mutters yes or no. Mom tries her hardest to engage Abuela in a conversation, mentioning San Antonio and the Mexican store where they used to buy their *masa,* only Abuela remains detached. It's almost as if she's afraid to speak. I wonder what's running through her mind. I wonder if she remembers being lost this afternoon. Probably not.

At midnight, we sit around the artificial tree Mom puts up every year, and we exchange gifts. Dad grins when he opens his new monster wrench set from Sears. I'm sure he picked it out himself since he loves working on cars. And Mom likes the burgundy-colored ceramic set of bowls I gave her. "They're beautiful, *hijo.* I'll use them tomorrow," she smiles.

Manuel, who has been pouting ever since Mom told him they couldn't afford to get him the iPod, carefully examines his gifts—a pair of checkered pajamas, socks, and some new cologne I bought him. His face lights up when he opens the $30 gift certificate from Boo Boo Records. "I'll get the new Usher CD with this," he says, sounding pleased.

I'm the next one to open my presents. When I come to the bottle of Sinful cologne Mom gave me, I exclaim, "I'll unleash Juanita's passion with this stuff!"

When Manuel tries to take it from me, I push his hand away, saying, "*Chale*—this isn't for babies—it's for real men." By now, Mom and Dad are laughing at the two of us.

We turn to gaze at Abuela, who has finally opened one of her presents. Abuela stares at the blue sheepskin slippers Mom picked out for her at Mervyn's as if she doesn't know what to do with them, so I tell her, "Nice *chanclas*—try them on, see if they fit."

Abuela nods, bending down to slip out of her old ones and into the new pair, which fit her perfectly. When she opens the porcelain angel I bought for her at work, she says, "*Está gordito*." Next, Mom hands her a large box. It is a brightly colored afghan.

"I made it for you, to keep you warm," Mom says, arranging it neatly around Abuela's stooped shoulders.

The last gift is from Manuel. It is a large gray pot holder shaped like a shark. Manuel puts it on, waving his right hand in the air. "See, Abuela, for when you help Mom cook."

"*Es un tiburón*," Abuela says, her eyes twinkling like neon lights. Now there are tears in Mom's eyes and I think back to the vibrant young woman in the photograph standing next to my grandfather on their wedding day.

FOURTEEN

Juanita calls me the minute she gets home from Christmas mass to invite me for some of her Amá's tamales. I don't have the heart to tell her I just had some for lunch and that I'm starting to get sick of tamales. Making sure I don't forget the crystal vase with the single red rose that I bought for her, I head out the door. I'm sure Juanita thinks I didn't buy her anything for Christmas, but when I saw it at Discount Foods, I knew it would be the perfect gift. Juanita's constantly saying how romantic it is when a girl gets flowers from a guy and that her Apá never bought flowers for her mom once in Juanita's life.

Mr. Chávez is out in front raking leaves when I arrive. We talk for a few minutes in Spanish, then he informs me that Juanita is expecting me. It's hard to believe that last year I still had to sneak around to see Juanita, and now Mr. Chávez actually approves of our dating. It makes me almost glad that Celia got pregnant, but I know I shouldn't think of it like that.

Before I can even knock, Markey flings the door open, saying, "She's in the kitchen with Amá." He's holding two new G.I. Joes in his right hand.

"Did Santo Clos bring you those?" I ask, stepping inside the entry way.

"Yes," Markey mutters and grabs my hand, pulling me toward his G.I. Joe fort which he's moved to the dining room, but I explain I have to see Juanita first. Celia, who looks bigger every time I see her, hollers out a hello from the living room where she and Rosario are working on a puzzle. Rosario, the second oldest of the three little ones (as Juanita calls them) waves as I walk past them to the kitchen. "*Buenos días*," I greet Mrs. Chávez, who is at the stove steaming tamales with Juanita's help.

"*¿Cómo estás,* Rodolfo*?*" Mrs. Chávez says, ordering Juanita to serve me some tamales.

"Amá's specialty—hope you're hungry," Juanita says, setting a plate of steaming tamales in front of me.

"Isn't anybody else eating?" I ask, and Lupita suddenly appears at the table, saying she's hungry too.

"Get out of here, *mocosa*," Juanita orders her. "You can eat later."

"You get out of here," Lupita snarls back. This year Lupita is nine years old, and according to Juanita, she's already acting like a Latina Barbie, prissy as hell. Juanita's horrified that Lupita is even beginning to obsess about her weight as if she were one of those anorexic models.

Mrs. Chávez sternly interrupts, reminding Lupita that she needs to clean the bathroom upstairs. Lupita turns to leave, but not before she glares at her sister.

"These tamales are delicious," I tell Mrs. Chávez in Spanish, explaining that Mom also makes them every year. Her face flushed from the heat of the stove, Mrs.

Chávez thanks me. As she places the last batch of tamales to steam, Mrs. Chávez reminds Juanita to serve me some more tamales. Then she politely excuses herself to go check on Lupita's cleaning.

Now that we're alone, I reach across the table and kiss Juanita on the lips. Returning my kiss, Juanita says, "Mmm, you taste like a *tamal.*"

"Baby, you better watch out—I'm super *enchilado*!"

Smiling, Juanita asks, "What's everyone doing on Christmas day at your house?"

"Keeping the doors locked."

"The doors locked?" Juanita repeats, her eyes widening like two full moons.

"Yeah, Abuela got lost yesterday. But I don't want to talk about it. Let's go for a drive."

"Okay, but are you sure you got enough to eat? Amá warned me to feed you well."

"Are you kidding? I ate six tamales! You want me to be a *panzón* like my dad?"

Juanita giggles as we go into the living room where her mom and Celia are on the couch watching *El Gordo y la Flaca*'s Christmas program. They're interviewing Paulina Rubio, who is wearing a sexy pair of shorts that look more like underwear. Rosario and Lupita are sitting in front of the TV mesmerized by their new Latina idol. "Stop drooling," Celia tells me, and I pretend to cover my eyes for a moment.

Markey is suddenly at my side, reminding me that I promised to play with him. "Go ahead—I'll be right back," Juanita says, turning to go upstairs.

I follow Markey to his G.I. Joe fort, and he shows me the different battle stations that are preparing for an attack. I'm totally engrossed in one of Markey's G.I. Joe operations when Juanita reappears, holding a Santa gift bag in her hand. "I'm ready whenever you are," she says, so I say my goodbye to Markey, who barely notices since he's in the midst of a bloody battle.

As we turn to leave, Juanita's mother reminds her to check in with her dad while Celia wistfully says, "Wish I could go out for a drive."

Lupita follows us to the door, asking if she can go with us, but Juanita simply shuts the door in her face. "That was mean," I say as we step outside, only Juanita scoffs at my remark. Mr. Chávez immediately gives her permission to go out, but not before he reminds me to drive carefully.

The moment we're in the front seat, I make Juanita close her eyes, then I place the vase with the rose in her hands. Opening her eyes, Juanita exclaims, "It's beautiful—thank you!" Then she gives me a fat juicy kiss on the lips.

We're driving away from the curb when we meet up with Carlos in his black Toyota. He honks and as we wave back, Juanita says, "Carlos has a new girlfriend. He met her at night school."

"That's cool. I didn't know he was back in school."

"Yeah, he's working on his GED . . . then he wants to go to Laguna College. Apá's real happy about it."

Today, Lakeside Park is practically empty, so we're able to park in a nice spot near the pier. There's a couple near the water's edge with their little boy, who is feeding bread crumbs to the ducks. Juanita hands me the gift bag she's been trying to hide from me. "*Feliz Navidad*," she says as I pull out a white teddy bear wearing a Santa hat. "He's cuddly like you!" Juanita grins, exposing her two giant dimples.

"Thanks, I'll put him next to my bed, but I sure wish it were you instead."

Juanita blushes as I pull her into my arms and we begin to make out. When my hand slowly edges up her blouse, Juanita pushes it away, saying, "Don't, Rudy. Come on, let's go for a walk."

Frustrated, I'm tempted to try again, but I know how stubborn Juanita can be. She's made it clear a hundred times that she won't have sex until we're married. Juanita says she doesn't want to end up like Celia. I guess a guy has to respect her for that. Besides, I'm too young to be a dad and, knowing her father, he'd beat the crap out of me if I got her pregnant.

We stroll alongside the water's edge, pausing to watch a solitary duck frantically wade toward the flock of ducks which are headed for the west end of the lake. Juanita's question forces me away from the lonely duck, "Aren't you going to tell me what happened with your grandma?"

"No big thing," I shrug. "She got lost. Some lady found her, took her to the cops. We brought her home."

"Is she all right?"

"Sort of, but it's hard to tell. Sometimes she acts normal, and other times she's totally out of it."

"You really should talk to Maya's mom. They're getting home this week. I guess they had to put Maya's grandma in a nursing home."

"My mom would die if that happened."

"Yeah, it's real hard. Maya says her Mom can't stop crying."

The wind suddenly kicks in, and a few raindrops start to fall. "*Vámonos*," I tell Juanita, tightening my grip on her hand.

Back at the apartment, I find everyone in the living room watching the end of the Lakers game. "Who's up?" I ask, sinking onto the couch next to Mom and Abuela.

"Lakers are down by six, and there's only two minutes left," Manuel answers.

Dad, who is a die-hard Laker fan, says, "Don't worry, Kobe's got the ball." When Kobe makes a three-pointer, Manuel is on his feet clapping his hands loudly. Abuela attempts to imitate Manuel, clapping her hands and cheering profusely as if she understands, only the sad thing is she's clueless. Manuel looks at Abuela with disgust, but before he can mouth off, I tell him to shut his face. Now Dad orders us both to stop it as Mom softly instructs Abuela to sit down.

FIFTEEN

The following night, I'm walking into the apartment when I hear Dad's loud voice coming from the living room. *He must be off tomorrow*, I think, pausing to hear Dad's heated conversation with Mom. "You need to take her to see a doctor. Something is seriously wrong with her."

"She's old, that's all," Mom replies, but Dad is insistent.

"*Ay*, Laura, you know that's not true. And what if she takes off again like the other day? Don't you remember what my *compadre* told us? That she needs to see a neurologist. The same thing happened to his mother."

When Mom begins to cry, I rush into the living room and put my arms around her. Frustrated, Dad rises to his feet. "I'm going to bed. Maybe you can talk some sense into her."

Alone with Mom, I try to console her, "Don't cry. Everything will be all right."

Looking up at me, she says, "*Ay, m'ijo*. I know your dad's right. I have to take Amá to see a specialist. But I'm so afraid of what he might say."

Just then, I hear the front door opening and moments later, Manuel appears in front of us. He takes one look at us and rolls his eyes, asking, "What's wrong? Did she get lost again? I think you oughta put grandma in a rest home."

"Shut up and go to bed," I snap at Manuel, watching a few more tears slide down Mom's cheeks.

"I'm only trying to help," Manuel states defiantly.

As he turns to leave, I tell Mom, "Manuel doesn't know what he's talking about. Don't listen to him."

"I know, *hijo.* But your dad's right."

"If it's the money you're worried about, I told you I can help."

Drawing in a deep breath, Mom shakes her head. "Amá has Medi-Cal." There is a moment of silence, then Mom admits, "I'm worried about how Amá will react. She's always hated going to the doctor. I remember the time she was having those fainting spells. Your Tío Manuel practically had to tie her up to get her to see a doctor."

Forcing a smile, I say, "I can't blame Abuela for that. No one likes going to the doctor."

"Then she hardly speaks English anymore. All she wants to use is her Spanish. The doctor won't even be able to understand her."

"Maybe they have a bilingual nurse." But the moment I say this, I know that Mom's fear is very real. Even at Discount Foods where I work, there is only one other person besides me who speaks Spanish—Marta, who works in the deli. Then with all the immigrant-bashing that's going on, Mom's right to worry. I can't count all the times at Discount Foods that people make fun of someone who comes into the store and can't speak English. It makes me so mad. One time I wanted to punch this man in the face when I overheard him telling his wife, "Damn wetbacks. They ought to go back to Mexico if they don't want to learn English." It took everything in me to control my anger and pretend I didn't hear.

"Mom, if you want, I can go with you when you take Abuela to the doctor." I finally say, hoping to reassure her.

The dark clouds in Mom's eyes suddenly brighten. "Would you, *m'ijo*? I know the garbage company won't give your dad a day off that easily."

"Just let me know as soon as you can, so I can tell the manager."

Mom grabs my hand, thanking me as I turn toward the stairway.

When I open the door to my room, Manuel is on the floor listening to his stupid music. I reach down to rip the earphones off his head. "Cut it out, Rudy," he growls.

Moving to my side of the room, I kick off my shoes, demanding, "Lights out! I work tomorrow. Why were you such a dumb ass with Mom? Didn't you see she was crying?"

His face flushed, Manuel says, "I was only telling her the truth. Grandma needs to be put away. She's crazy."

"If anyone's crazy, it's you," I holler back. "Where *were* you anyway?"

"None of your business," Manuel grunts, heading into the bathroom.

"Selfish little punk," I whisper under my breath. All he thinks about is himself. One of these days I'm going to teach him a lesson he won't forget.

The next morning, I'm having this weird dream about a UFO landing in the school parking lot, when the alarm suddenly wakes me up. I hurry out of bed, glancing at Manuel, who is hidden under the covers sound asleep. Irritated that Manuel gets to sleep, I purposely make a lot of noise in the bathroom, banging the cabinet doors. Manuel doesn't budge at all. It's the pits having to work during Christmas break, I think to myself, slamming the bedroom door behind me and going downstairs to eat breakfast. As soon as I clock in at Discount Foods, Stella, the manager, who is working at one of the registers since we're shorthanded, calls me over to bag groceries for her. When a frail-looking old lady slowly maneuvers her cart up to the counter, I wonder if she has enough strength to take everything out of her cart. I move quickly to help her.

"Thank you, young man," she says, gazing at me with her dull gray eyes.

As I go back behind the counter to bag her groceries, I notice the two college guys lining up behind her. They are carrying a twelve-pack of beer and a giant bag of Doritos. When the little old lady takes out her leather coin purse and meticulously counts out the exact change, the tall red-faced guy mutters under his breath, "Hurry up, Granny." His friend laughs as they edge closer to the old lady, almost crowding her out.

Flashing a disgusted look toward the two guys, Stella thanks the lady for handing her the exact change.

I glare at the two idiots, wishing I could spit on them, but Stella saves the day. Thrusting a sign that says "closed" on the counter, she says, "Sorry, this register is closed. You'll have to go to another one."

The tall guy's face is contorted as he tells Stella that he's going to complain to the manager. Bemused, Stella says, "Guess what . . . I *am* the manager."

Stella and I exchange a satisfied glance as the two idiots walk away, cussing loudly at us.

That afternoon when I get home, Mom and Abuela are in the kitchen preparing dinner. "Smells good," I compliment them, and Abuela smiles up at me from the stove where she is stirring a huge pot.

"We're making chicken *mole*. It's Amá's recipe. She makes the best *mole* in the world." Then, moving closer to the doorway, Mom whispers, "I made the appointment for next Wednesday. Your dad can't go with me."

"I'll ask for the day off."

"Thanks, *m'ijo,*" Mom says, going back to the stove to keep an eye on Abuela.

Upstairs in my room, I'm glad Manuel's not around so I can turn the radio as loud as I want to on my favorite Spanish station. As I stretch my feet out on the bed, I think about Abuela's doctor's appointment. I sure hope Abuela doesn't freak on us. Maybe I better pump some more weights in case I need more muscle power. Just then, I remember I was supposed to call Juanita during my break and I forgot. Swinging my feet over the edge of the bed, I head for the door thinking I better call her right now or I'll never hear the end of it.

SIXTEEN

Mom's fearful thoughts turn out to be accurate. We practically have to drag Abuela into Dr. Mazelwick's office. Angry and sulking like a little kid, Abuela insists she'll wait for us in the car. "It only takes a few minutes," Mom begs in Spanish. Still, Abuela won't budge, so Mom raises her voice in frustration, saying, "Amá, we have to see the doctor. You know that something's wrong. You forget a lot of things. Dr. Mazelwick can help you."

Now the seriousness in Mom's voice seems to convince Abuela, so she reluctantly climbs out of the car. As we walk to the gray medical building, I know Abuela is frightened because her right eye is twitching badly. If she only knew that Mom's scared too, and that's why she insisted I come along. I can't imagine bringing Abuela here by myself.

We take the elevator to the third floor, and the moment we're inside Dr. Mazelwick's office, the receptionist greets us with a warm smile. "You must be Dolores. How are you today?" she asks Abuela, who responds with a hostile stare.

Smiling apologetically to the receptionist, I direct Abuela toward two empty chairs near the back while

Mom fills out the paper work. I hand Abuela a copy of *Woman's Day* off the table in front of us, hoping to defuse her anger. Then I study the brochures on the shelves across from where we're seated: "Women and Alzheimer's Disease," "Tips for Caregivers," and "Meeting the Challenges of Dementia." Feeling uneasy, I start to bite my nails. Juanita's always hammering on me that it's a bad habit, but today I can't help it.

As Mom joins us, a tall angelic-faced nurse comes into the room. Introducing herself as Ginny, she informs us that Dr. Mazelwick is ready to see Abuela. When Abuela refuses to get up, Mom pulls her on her feet, and Abuela swears in Spanish. We follow Ginny through a short hallway and into a large brightly decorated receiving room. "Those are cool," I tell Abuela, whose eyes are focused on the painting on the wall of a field of giant sunflowers.

"*Están feas*," Abuela says in Spanish as Dr. Mazelwick walks into the room.

Dr. Mazelwick reminds me of my math teacher in junior high. He has a long, narrow face with thin black hair. There are patches of gray at his temples, and he is wearing horn-rimmed glasses that look as if they are about to slide off his pointy nose. "Hello. I'm Dr. Mazelwick," he says, shaking hands with Mom. Dr. Mazelwick doesn't seem to be offended when Abuela rejects his handshake. Pulling up a stool, he carefully explains that he's going to ask Abuela a series of questions.

Mom nods as Dr. Mazelwick begins. "Can you tell me what your full name is?"

Fidgeting in her chair, Abuela answers defiantly, "Dolores Molinar Pérez."

Dr. Mazelwick then passes Abuela his clipboard, asking her to write her name out. When Abuela slowly copies her full name in what appears like a child's scribbling, Dr. Mazelwick compliments her for completing the task. Then he asks Abuela to repeat her birth date. Now Abuela hesitates, repeating the month, only she can't remember the day and year. By now Abuela's face is flushed, and she's anxiously clasping and unclasping her hands, but Dr. Mazelwick doesn't let up. "Dolores, can you tell me what day of the week this is?"

Waves of pity consuming me, I want to answer for Abuela, blurt out that it's Wednesday, tell Dr. Mazelwick that half the time I don't even know what day it is, especially during the holiday break. But Mom beats me to it. "She's a little confused about the time because she just moved here from Texas."

"I see," Dr. Mazelwick says, going on to ask Abuela if she knows the name of the President of the United States. Only Abuela can't seem to remember. Next, Dr. Mazelwick asks Abuela to spell "perception," then to spell it backwards. Abuela tries her hardest to spell back the word, but she mixes up all the letters and it comes out all messed up. Mom and I stare angrily at. Dr. Mazelwick. Doesn't he know that Abuela didn't even graduate from high school? How would he like it if we asked him to spell Guadalajara or Michoacán?

In a calm, mild manner, Dr. Mazelwick thanks Abuela for trying, then he asks her to close her eyes and touch her nose with her index finger. "Well done, Dolores," he compliments Abuela, who completes the task successfully. Only now, Abuela stiffens, appearing more uncomfortable by the minute. When Dr. Mazelwick turns to Mom and asks who is taking care of Abuela, I hear Mom tell a lie for the first time in my life. By now, Abuela is shaking, and I can't blame her since Dr. Mazelwick is acting as if she is invisible.

"I'm with her most of the time. If I have to go out, I leave her with a neighbor."

Satisfied, Dr. Mazelwick explains his diagnosis, "Dolores has progressive dementia. Eventually, she will need to be hospitalized." Then he moves toward a cabinet and returns with some samples, handing them to Mom, who seems paralyzed by the sudden news. "Here are some samples of the most recent drugs being used today to help slow the disease."

Suddenly, Abuela curses loudly in Spanish and rushes out of the room. Grabbing the keys from Mom, I hurry after Abuela, guiding her back past the reception area and out to the elevator. Abuela is furious at the doctor, "Does he think I'm stupid?" she repeats as we arrive at the main floor, making our way out to the car.

By the time Mom returns to the car, Abuela has stopped shaking, but she begins to accuse Mom of trying to put her away in a nursing home. When Abuela succumbs to a flurry of tears, Mom reaches over and holds her tightly until she's only whimpering. Then Mom asks, "Amá, how about some ice cream?"

The dullness in Abuela's eyes disappears for a moment. "I want chocolate fudge," she happily agrees, as Mom instructs me to drive by Baskin Robbins.

"I'll take a strawberry shake," I join in, turning on the ignition as Abuela begins to talk about her *comadre* Inés in San Antonio.

By the time I clock in at Discount Foods, the store is already jam-packed with customers. As I bag up the groceries for a distraught woman with a pair of noisy twins, my thoughts drift to Dr. Mazelwick's final words and the fear in Mom's eyes. When a dozen eggs slip out of my hands and crash to the floor, I'm brought back to the present moment. Calling me a klutz, Myrna apologizes to the customer and orders me to retrieve her a new dozen. Hurrying toward the dairy section, I wonder if maybe I *should* call Maya's mom and tell her about Abuela.

SEVENTEEN

Professor Sonia Gonzales

We finally arrived in Laguna around midnight after being delayed at LAX for almost two hours due to fog. Glenn was there to pick us up, looking handsome and relaxed from his Christmas break. When he asked about Mom, I hesitated, recounting our final visit and how she'd begged me to take her home again.

"But the nurse said Grandma will get used to it, that they all do that," Maya added as Glenn offered some words of comfort.

On the ten-minute drive from the airport, Maya rambled on about her cousins in Santa Fe. Glenn interrupted several times to ask a few questions, but for the most part he listened patiently to Maya's animated description of our New Mexican Christmas, complete with Tía Lola's tamales and the tree-lighting in the plaza.

As soon as we turned into Laguna Heights, Maya cried out, "Yeah! Home sweet home! I can hardly wait to see Ty!"

Once he was finished bringing in our luggage, Glenn pulled me into his arms, saying, "It's late, and you need some sleep." We exchanged a long kiss before he left, promising to call tomorrow.

I was dreaming that I was racing up and down the aisles of a huge department store frantically searching for Mom when the jingle on my cell phone suddenly awakened me. "Welcome back, stranger," Sandra greeted me cheerfully. "How was the flight?"

It took me a few moments to register that I was back home in my own bed before I was able to reply. "Horrid. We didn't get home until after midnight."

"Due to the fog, I'm sure. Listen, are you up for lunch at My Lin's today"

"Yes, that would be nice," I agreed, thinking that besides being a shrink, Sandra had to be psychic. I must have thought of her at least five or six times during the flight home.

"Great. I'll see you there in an hour."

Glancing at the alarm clock, I jumped out of bed and took a long, hot shower. Though I missed Mom terribly, it was comforting to be back home, and if I ever needed to talk with my best friend, it was now.

Sandra was waiting for me at a booth near the window. Embracing me, she said, "I've missed my favorite *comadre.*"

"Me too," I replied, taking a seat across from her as the waiter appeared with a pot of tea.

Her eyes burning into me, Sandra said, "You look terrible. Have you lost some weight?"

"Gee, thanks," I winced.

"Seriously, are you all right?"

The words came rushing out of my mouth. "No, Sandy, of course not. My appetite's gone. I haven't slept in weeks. I keep having these terrible dreams about Mom, that she's lost and I can't find her."

Sandra leaned forward, patting my hand as the waiter reappeared to take our order. As soon as we were alone, she asked, "Have you thought about getting some help, maybe attending an Alzheimer's Support Group?"

I took a deep breath. "I don't know—I need to get ready for next quarter."

Sandra's intense stare made me shift uncomfortably in my seat. "I know how busy you are, but you need to make time for this. There are a variety of support groups in Laguna, and they're held at different times. I'm sure one of them will fit into your schedule."

"Do you really think a support group would help? Wouldn't it make me feel worse listening to other depressing situations like Mom's?"

"I know it would help," Sandra insisted. "Alzheimer's is a terrible disease. It's like a long death, and the family members or caregivers are the ones that suffer the most."

We grew quiet as the waiter reappeared with two steaming bowls of War Won Ton Soup. "There's also an Alzheimer's website," Sandra continued. "Why don't you check it out? I have clients who often talk about the invaluable information it provided for them. Maya might even like it since it's online."

Recognizing how convenient it was to have a psychologist for a best friend, I finally shrugged, "Okay. I'll check it out today."

Sandra smiled. "You won't regret it."

By the time Glenn arrived that evening, I had already spent several hours researching the Alzheimer's website. I was shocked to find out that more than four million Americans suffered from Alzheimer's or a form of dementia. Another article that had caught my attention discussed the increased risk of Alzheimer's disease among Hispanics and African Americans. Over dinner, I quoted from one of the articles I'd printed out: "Among Hispanics in the United States, during the first half of the twenty-first century, Alzheimer's disease and related dementia are projected to increase more than six-fold. This means that 1.3 million Hispanics will have Alzheimer's disease by 2050, compared to fewer than 200,000 currently living with the disease."

"I never would have imagined that," Glenn said.

"They also give updates on the latest research, new drugs they're trying. I feel so guilty. I should have researched this a long time ago—maybe I could've helped Mom more."

Glenn reached across the table for my hand. "Sweetheart, don't feel guilty. You did the best you could."

"I only wish I'd known all of this before, paid more attention to Mom's worsening illness," I whispered.

We were listening to Los Lobos' newest CD when Maya appeared in the family room with Rudy and Tyrone at her side. "Hey, Glenn," Maya said, turning to look at me. "Mom, Rudy was wondering if he could talk to you."

"Of course," I answered. While Maya introduced Glenn to a nervous Rudy, I exchanged a few words with Tyrone about the Teen Center.

After a few minutes, Glenn reached for his keys on the table, saying, "Time to go. I promised to help out early in the morning with the MEChA car wash."

I walked Glenn to the door, and when I returned, I found Maya showing off her tennis trophies on the mantel to Rudy and Tyrone. "Maya's quite a jock!" Tyrone said.

Maya giggled, pulling Tyrone toward the stairway. "Ty and I are going upstairs to my room so you and Rudy can talk."

Narrowing my eyes, I warned, "Make sure you keep that door open."

"Oh, Mom, what do you think we're gonna do? Have sex?" Maya hollered back as they left the room.

Grimacing, I invited Rudy to take a seat on the couch, wondering what could be on his mind. "How's Juanita?" I asked, hoping to get him to relax.

"Bossy," Rudy grinned. After an uncomfortable pause, he continued. "She said I should talk to you about my grandma. She's sick like your Mom—real sick. She got lost one day, so Mom decided to take her to see a specialist. He said she has Alzheimer's."

Gazing intensely at Rudy's troubled face, I replied, "I see. How is your Mom handling all of this?"

Rudy shook his head sadly. "She cries all the time. She goes off the deep end for any little thing."

I was struck by Rudy's words. They sounded all too familiar. Sadness. Anxiety. Fear. "What about you?" I asked, fixing my gaze back on Rudy.

"Me? I'm fine. But my brother Manuel's been acting weird. I think he's the one who's freaked."

"I didn't know you had a brother. How old is he?"

"He's fourteen, but he acts like he's twenty."

A sudden thought entered my mind. "Rudy, would you, Manuel, and your Mom like to attend an Alzheimer's support group meeting with me this week? If you'd like, I can call your mom."

Fidgeting with the zipper on his jacket, Rudy asked, "Is Maya going?"

"I haven't mentioned it to her yet, but yes, I'll think she'll want to come."

Rudy was quiet for a moment. "Yeah, I'll go, but I don't know if my mom or Manuel will want to."

"Well, all I can do is try," I answered, wishing I could protect Rudy and his family from all the grief that awaited them.

EIGHTEEN

Professor Sonia Gonzales

As we pulled into the parking lot of the small Presbyterian church, Rudy apologized from the backseat for his mother's stubbornness. "I tried to invite Manuel too, but he wouldn't listen."

Glancing at Rudy through the rearview mirror, I told him reassuringly, "It's all right. I understand." I had called Mrs. Ortiz, but she had politely refused to attend the Alzheimer's support group meeting, offering a number of excuses. Yet, how could I be critical of Rudy's family when I myself had been in denial for years about Mom's illness? If only I had listened to Tía Lola when she stated that Mom could no longer make out a grocery list or balance her checking account. I'd rationalized all of it as old age, unaware that they were signs of early memory failure.

"I'm so glad you came with us," Maya told Rudy, interrupting my guilty thoughts. "This way I won't be the only one with all those *viejitos*."

"Better watch who you're calling a *viejita*!" I teased, noticing the half-smile appearing on Rudy's handsome face.

We climbed out of the car and made our way to the entrance of the church where a sign had been placed, pointing us in the direction of tonight's meeting. Inside, we were greeted by a large woman with sharp blue eyes who introduced herself as Tess, the group facilitator. She was standing next to a table covered with variety of pamphlets and books on dementia and Alzheimer's. There were several copies of *Alzheimer's, A Caregiver's Guide and Sourcebook*, which I'd seen listed on the Alzheimer's website.

Handing each of us a nametag, Tess suggested, "Help yourself to any of our informational brochures."

When I thanked Tess, explaining that it was our first time, she smiled and pointed to the large meeting room to her left. "I'm glad you came. There are still some empty chairs."

Following another couple that was just arriving, we took a seat in the back row of the brightly colored room. All of the chairs were arranged in a semi-circle, and there were signs on the walls which indicated that this room was also used for daycare activities. Glancing around, I noticed that most of the participants were middle-aged or older.

"You were right—we're the youngest ones here," Rudy whispered to Maya.

"See, Mom, I told you," Maya said, and I reminded them both that they didn't have to participate, only listen.

At exactly seven o'clock, Tess approached the front of the group, welcoming everyone to the meeting. She then asked for all the newcomers to raise their hands. Maya nudged Rudy until he reluctantly raised his hand. I noticed that the pixie-faced woman several chairs to my right also raised her hand. Our eyes meeting, we hastily repeated our names out loud. Her name was Sherry Wilcox.

Maya had to give Rudy another slight jab in order to get him to say his name. I could tell he was nervous from the uneven tilt of his voice.

Taking a seat, Tess promptly asked, "Is there anyone that would like to begin?"

Almost instantly, the slight thin-faced woman in the front row began to speak. "I'm at the end of my rope. I think my husband is going to divorce me if I don't do something, but every time I try to talk to Mom about a care facility, she threatens to kill herself."

The woman to her left, wearing a pair of long beaded earrings said, "My mother used to say that to us. Then she got worse and forgot all about it. But it was very frightening at the time."

There were dark shadows in the thin woman's eyes. "It's so dam hard," she continued. "I think it's even affecting my kids. My son Michael's grades dropped. He's flunking out of ninth grade."

Tess measured each word carefully. "Leslie, there are different stages of grief that each family member goes through which are similar to the stages of adjustment to death. Therefore, it's common for young people to react in different ways when a family member has Alzheimer's.

Sometimes they fear that the disease is contagious or worry that their parents might get it. It's important to talk to them, let them express their fears."

I caught Maya's eyes. I knew we were both thinking about how I'd tried to conceal my fears and hurt from her, especially while in New Mexico. Now I knew I'd done the right thing in taking her with me and letting her help me take Mom to the nursing home.

Turning to the lady next to her, Tess asked, "Linda, how's Mike doing?"

Linda took a deep breath, tucking a loose strand of wavy hair behind her ear before she answered. "Last week, Mike insisted I take him to his office. He keeps forgetting he no longer has one. But he begged and begged, so I finally gave in, but when he got to campus, he couldn't remember where his office was, so he became very agitated. He started to cuss me out." Linda's voice broke, and we waited until she was able to continue. "Mike takes all his anger out on me, but I know it's not his fault. It's so hard, he's only fifty-seven. He used to be one of the most active professors, reading, lecturing. Now he can't remember anything he reads."

With a heavy sigh, Linda bowed her head as Tess patted her gently on the shoulder. Sherry was the next one to speak. "I moved here from Boston to help Mom with Dad. It was too difficult being that far away, so I left my job, my home. It's a good thing I'm divorced, because I have no social life. I'm physically exhausted helping Mom care for Dad twenty-four/seven. And it's frustrating as hell. Sometimes I feel as if I'm going to explode.

Dad got lost the other day. He wandered off, and we had to call the police."

Rudy whispered something in Maya's ear. I imagined it was about the recent episode with his grandmother.

"It would be very helpful to get your father an identification bracelet," Tess explained to Sherry. "This month's newsletter, which I've brought for each of you, includes the website address where you can obtain one."

"I didn't know there was such a thing," Sherry admitted.

Straightening in my chair, I felt inspired to speak. "I know exactly how you feel," I said, glancing at Sherry. "My mom lives in New Mexico, and I finally had to put her in a care facility. It's been very frustrating all these years being so far away from her."

"It's hell either way," Sherry agreed.

An olive-skinned woman with hollow eyes leaned forward in her chair, her shoulders slumped. "I just can't take it any more. I have high blood pressure. Mom is mean to us—my brother and I take care of her. All she does is curse at us, call us names. The other day she spit on me. I think I'm gonna have a stroke one of these days."

"I thought my mom was depressed," Rudy muttered to Maya, who nodded in agreement.

"Self-care is extremely important for caregivers," Tess responded. Then, on her feet, she began to pass out copies of the Alzheimer's Association Newsletter along with a bright green brochure. "In this pamphlet, you'll find some important tips for caregivers. Please read them carefully. Rule Number One clearly states, 'A caregiver must take care of herself first.' You can also obtain a free CD from the Alzheimer's website that contains a caregiver manual to help you learn the critical techniques of care giving. Caring for someone with Alzheimer's requires special skills and a specific attitude. I encourage all caregivers to obtain a copy of this CD. And for those of you who are new to our meetings, we have an excellent daycare program that even provides transportation. It gives caregivers a chance to take time out for themselves—to go out for lunch with a friend, get a massage."

"That would be a dream come true," Sherry exclaimed, and several women quickly agreed with her.

Sounding defeated, the olive-skinned woman confessed, "Mom refuses to leave the house."

Tess calmly replied, "I know it's hard, but you'd be surprised at all the different strategies you can use to get them out the door. Once they get to daycare, they actually like it. Please contact someone at the Alzheimer's hotline, and they'll help you discuss the right way to get your loved one to attend. Remember, self care is important for the duration of the disease."

Tess promptly brought the meeting to an end. I was about to ask Rudy and Maya what they thought, when they jumped to their feet and headed out the doorway.

NINETEEN

Rudy

Early the next morning, Stella the manager calls from Discount Foods to say that one of the baggers called in sick. Since it's New Year's Eve, she asks if I can come in right away, so I rush to get dressed. I hitch a ride with Mom, who is on her way to work at the Coral Inn. When I ask if she's not worried about Abuela taking off like the last time, Mom sighs, "She was still asleep when we left, and I told Manuel to keep an eye on her. I also get off early today. I told Amá I'd help her make *capirotada.*"

Thinking back to last night's group meeting, I say, "They have identification bracelets you can get for someone like Abuela in case they get lost."

"She'll be fine," Mom curtly replies as if she's not interested.

At Discount Foods, I clock in, waving at Tyrone's dad as I go past the meat department. I go straight to Matt's station where he's ringing up a customer. "Glad you're here," he says. "It's going to be one of those days."

There is a steady flow of customers all morning long, but it's the overwrought mothers with their spoiled brats that slow the lines down. It makes me wonder why parents bring their kids to the store when all they do is scream their heads off, wanting everything they see. When I have kids, I'm never taking them to the store—I'll lock them up in their rooms and let them cry.

During my lunch break, I walk across the street to Subway for an Italian meatball sandwich. Then I sit outside at one of their cement tables and for the very first time, I catch myself observing all the old people. Some of them look way older than Abuela, but they're still out shopping and driving their own cars. I wonder if Abuela would be as independent as them if she hadn't gotten sick.

By afternoon, the store gets even more packed with people stopping by on their way home from work. Eggnog is a top-selling item, along with bottles of liquor. At five, I'm clocking out to leave when Mr. Cameron comes by to offer me a ride home. As we walk out to his old Buick, I ask him about his New Year's celebration. "We're gonna stay home just like old folks," he says, "watch the countdown on TV at Times Square. No booze for me this year."

"That's cool," I answer, remembering how skeptical Tyrone felt when his dad first mentioned A.A. It took months before Tyrone finally realized his dad was determined to change. That's cool for Mr. Cameron, I think to myself as he asks what my parents will be doing. "Same as you," I answer, "only they'll probably watch the New Year's stuff on Univisión."

In a few minutes, we're driving through the city streets, and as we turn on to Cabrillo Street, Mr. Cameron says, "Tyrone said you're all invited to a party tonight?"

"Yeah . . . at Ankiza's. It'll be sweet."

"You all be careful now," Mr. Cameron advises, pulling up in front of our apartment. "A lot of crazies out tonight."

"We will," I answer, thanking him again as I shut the door behind me.

Abuela is in the dining room, and I want to laugh because she's ironing a pair of her baggy *calzones*. "Manuel, *hijo*," she says, looking up at me.

"I'm Rudy," I explain, impulsively kissing her wrinkled cheek.

Just then, Mom walks out of the kitchen. "*Hijo*, Amá and I made some *capirotada*. Would you like some?"

"Sí, Manuel have some *capirotada*," Abuela eagerly agrees. Mom and I exchange a smile while Abuela rambles on about how my grandfather Manuel loved *capirotada* so much that he wouldn't stop eating it until his stomach ached.

Waiting until she's finished, I tell Mom, "I'll have some later. I have to shower and get ready to pick up Juanita. Can I borrow your car tonight?"

"Sure, *hijo*, but you'll need to get some gas."

"Thanks, Mom," I answer, heading upstairs to my room.

Manuel is lying on his bed reading one of my Cucaracha comic books while he listens to music. "Turn that down," I demand, wondering why he can't listen to *rancheras* or oldies instead of all that hip-hop. As I fling my sneakers into the closet, I notice the crumpled up paper on the floor. Picking it up, I realize it's Manuel's semester grade report. There are four Ds and an F. Angry, I wave the grade report in his face.

"How does a person get an F in P.E.? Are you some kind of *pendejo*?"

When Manuel grunts, I quickly grab my comic book out of his hands. Now Manuel's eyes are bulging out with anger. "What's your problem? I just had a bad quarter, that's all," he says, his cheeks flushed.

"What's going on? You think I'm stupid? No one gets four Ds and an F for nothing."

Reaching for his sneakers, Manuel says, "I suppose now you're gonna tell Mom and Dad?"

"Why shouldn't I?"

"Who cares anyway?" Manuel shouts back, getting up to leave before I can get an explanation out of him.

As soon as she sees me at the door, Lupita obnoxiously yells, "Juanita your boyfriend's here."

It's no wonder Juanita complains about Lupita's big mouth, I think to myself as I go inside to greet Markey, who eagerly states in his little boy's voice, "Los Reyes Magos are bringing me presents."

"They're bringing me some too," Rosario happily adds, entering the room with Juanita.

"Better say hello to my dad first," Juanita warns, leading me into the living room where Mr. Chávez is watching *El Gordo y La Flaca*'s New Year's Eve fiesta.

As I greet Mr. Chávez, I can feel needles prickling my neck. He asks for my parents, and I explain that they're probably watching the same holiday show.

From there, we go into the kitchen, and I'm surprised to find Carlos sitting at the table eating tamales with the three little ones. "How's work?" I ask, declining Mrs. Chávez's invitation to eat.

"It sucks," Carlos says, going on to complain about his erratic schedule. Then his face brightens as he talks about the night classes he's taking for his GED.

"Now everyone in our family will graduate," Mrs. Chávez beams with pride.

When Juanita offers me some *champurrado*, I ask, "What's that?"

Rosario and Markey giggle while Lupita rudely exclaims, "Don't tell me you're Mexican and you've never heard of *champurrado*?"

Juanita glares at Lupita, explaining that *champurrado* is a typical drink that's made of Mexican chocolate and *masa*. "Amá always makes it for the holidays."

"Doesn't your mom make *champurrado*?" Rosario innocently asks.

Shaking my head, I explain that Mom makes *capirotada* for Christmas and New Year's. Lupita frowns, but Mrs. Chávez comes to my defense.

"It's delicious," she says in Spanish. "I had some last year at my *comadre* Marta's—she's from Tejas too."

Juanita suddenly interrupts, pulling me toward the doorway. "Rudy, let's go or we'll be late for the party."

"Wish I could go to a party," Celia sighs wistfully.

Carlos laughs, shaking his head. “No more parties for you. Your time’s going be spent changing diapers and fixing bottles.”

Celia scoffs while snotty Lupita smiles facetiously.

TWENTY

Ankiza lives a few blocks away from Maya in Laguna Hills, which is a professional neighborhood with luxurious homes. It must be nice—a big fancy home and parents that trust you, though Ankiza told Juanita she had to beg her parents to agree to the party. They also made it very clear they'd only be a few blocks away at a neighbor's New Year's Eve party.

Sheena answers the door when we get there. "Hey, *mosco*!" she says, hugging Juanita. I can hear music from upstairs.

"Your Spanish is about as ugly as Mrs. Plumb," I tease her back as we follow her up the walnut stairway.

I've never been inside Ankiza's house before, so when we get to the family room, I check out the cathedral ceilings and huge bay window where you can see one of Laguna's breath-taking peaks. Garland and stockings hang from the marble fireplace, as well as a huge banner that reads "Happy New Year."

Ankiza is in the middle of the room dancing with Rina and Donovan, but the moment she sees us, she moves to our side. "I'm glad you're here. Hope you're hungry. The pizza is on its way."

I flick my chin up to greet Donovan, ignoring Rina who yells out, "Mosco Man!"

Donovan is one of the most popular African Americans at our school and lately he's been walking around campus a lot with Rina Schwarzenegger. Juanita says Rina has a thing for him, the poor guy.

"Ready to dance?" Ankiza asks, but I shake my head She points to the living room. "Maya and Tyrone are playing videogames."

"That's cool," I eagerly state, but Juanita pulls me away toward the fireplace where Marsea Grant is standing next to her boyfriend Tyler. Marsea is this year's senior class president. She's pretty cool. Last year, she stuck up big time for Ankiza when someone wrote a racist letter and left it at Ankiza's locker. Marsea knows what it's like to be treated different since she's Jewish.

While Juanita and Marsea talk about graduation, Tyler and I compare notes on the Laker's winning season. Tyler was in my Econ class last semester, but I've never really hung out with him. When Sheena approaches us insisting we dance, I finally escape to the living room, leaving Juanita behind to dance. Glancing up at me from the floor, Maya says, "You can take over now . . . Tyrone's beating my butt."

Tyrone calls Maya a coward as I grab the joystick from her hand before she leaves the room.

Soon I'm battling it out with Tyrone, and I'm about to kill him off when Maya reappears with Juanita, announcing that the pizza has arrived. "I'll get you next time," I warn Tyrone as Juanita jerks my arm hard.

"That's what you think," Tyrone grins.

Minutes later, Juanita and I take our pizza over to the couch to join Rina and Donovan. "Where's Tommy?" I ask Ankiza who is sitting on the edge of the fireplace next to Sheena.

"He's crashing another party," she answers. Then Maya explains that one of Tommy's friends from the Gay Pride Alliance invited him to a New Year's Eve celebration at his home.

"That's cool," Tyrone says in between mouthfuls.

When Marsea asks what everyone is doing for spring break, Sheena almost chokes on her food. "Who can afford to go anywhere? Not me."

"Tell me about it," Rina agrees. "I'm going to salsa at the Golden Arches Club!" I have to smile at the image of Rina flipping burgers while dancing salsa at McDonalds.

"Dad wants to take us on a cruise," Ankiza sighs. "Athena's excited, but I told him I won't go. I don't want to get seasick."

"You can get pills for that," Donovan suggests, recounting how last summer he took them during the Caribbean cruise with his parents. "I never once got seasick."

Ankiza nods, turning to Juanita. "Are you doing anything for break?"

Sighing, Juanita explains that she has to babysit the three little ones while her mom works. "And Celia's no help at all—all she wants to do is lay around."

Giggling, Maya asks me about my plans, and I answer, "Sticking close to home if that's what you mean."

When Tyrone asks if my grandma has gotten worse, I take a slow breath. "Yeah, sort of. I'm trying to help keep an eye on her."

Marsea sighs regretfully. "I wish my grandparents lived close by, but they're in New York. I only get to see them once or twice a year."

Tyler nods. "Yeah, me too. Mine live in Ohio."

Feeling the urge to change the topic of conversation, I ask Ankiza about Hunter, and she nonchalantly replies, "He's home for the break, only we're not dating anymore if that's what you mean. We're still friends, though."

I am about to ask why they broke up, but Juanita gives me a warning pinch, so instead, I concentrate on my last slice of pizza.

After we're done eating, Ankiza puts on Beyonce's newest CD, and Rina grabs Donovan by the hand to dance. "You too," she orders as Juanita pulls me to my feet.

As soon as the song ends, I escape to an empty chair near the fireplace, leaving Juanita to dance with Ankiza and Sheena—only my freedom is short-lived as Sheena rushes up to me and grabs my hand for the next song. "Come on, Rudy, let's shake it!"

Juanita giggles as I'm forced to dance with them, but after a few minutes, I beg off, saying I have to use the bathroom. Only I don't. I sneak over to the CD player and put on Los Tigres del Norte. Rina groans when a *norteña* comes on, but Maya sticks up for me. "My mom loves *norteñas*!" Then she and Tyrone join us as we dance a Mexican polka. Marsea and Tyler try to imitate us, only Tyler keeps stepping on Marsea's toes. We're jamming away to a fast *corrido* when the music abruptly switches to a weird hip-hop reggaeton beat that Manuel would probably like. Rina excitedly reveals that it is by the hottest Boricua group from Puerto Rico.

At around eleven-thirty, Sheena and Maya help Ankiza hand out colorful party hats, whistles, and confetti-filled eggs. As Ankiza sets out three champagne bottles of sparkling cider, Tyler retrieves a small bottle of vodka from the inside pocket of his denim jacket. Waving it in the air, he says, "Let's have a real toast!"

"All right!" I reply, but the moment the words come out of my mouth, I feel a sharp jab in my ribs from Juanita.

Maya responds quickly, grabbing the bottle out of Tyler's hand. "Haven't you heard of drunk drivers?" she glares at him.

Before Tyler can respond, Rina says, "This woman from MADD came to speak to us in Health Ed last semester. Her five-year-old daughter was killed by a drunk driver."

Her face flaming, Marsea apologizes, "Sorry, Ankiza. I didn't know Tyler had that."

"It's not your fault, Marsea. But I promised my parents no alcohol or drugs," Then Maya hands Tyler back his small bottle.

Only Tyler is persistent. "Not even for one toast?"

By now, Marsea is angry. "Grow up, Tyler!" she hisses, grabbing the bottle out of his hand and tossing it inside her purse.

Embarrassed, Tyler apologizes to Ankiza, then to Marsea who warns him not to try it again.

We have a countdown during the final minute, lifting our glasses high in the air to ring in the New Year. "Here's to graduation!" Ankiza exclaims.

Then Rina joins in, shouting, "To being free and independent!"

This is followed by another round of toasts. Sheena forcefully adds, "Here's to getting away from my mom!"

After several more toasts, I turn to Juanita and give her a long kiss on the lips. Then I take Rina by surprise and give her a quick kiss on the left cheek. Rubbing her cheek fiercely, a stunned Rina says, "*Híjole*! I hope I don't get a disease!" Laughter breaks out as we take turns hugging each other.

The party comes to an end when Ankiza's parents arrive shortly after midnight.

TWENTY-ONE

I'm unlocking the front door when Manuel suddenly appears behind me. His face is flushed and he is out of breath. "Don't tell me you're just getting home. If Dad finds out, you're in deep trouble."

"I was at Jordan's." Manuel mumbles, following me through the hallway and upstairs to my room.

Once the door is closed behind us and I'm certain no one can hear us, I turn to Manuel, raising my voice. "Now you are gonna tell me what the hell you were doing?"

I'm stunned when Manuel sinks onto the edge of his bed, bursting into tears. I haven't seen him cry since he was a little boy, and for a moment, I'm not sure what to do. Moving to his side, I ask, "What's going on?"

By now, Manuel is whimpering. He shakes his head, whispering, "Nothing."

Still, I know something is wrong for him to cry like a baby. Sitting next to him, I place my hand on his shoulder. "Come on, Manuel. Tell me what's wrong."

Lifting his head, Manuel looks straight at me, fear in his dark brown eyes. "Is Abuela gonna die?"

Manuel's question takes me by complete surprise. "I thought you couldn't stand having her around?"

Bowing his head, Manuel explains, "I know I've been mean to her, but I really do love Grandma."

I want to remind Manuel about his pissy behavior with Abuela ever since she arrived, but his remorse holds me back. "Abuela's sick, that's all."

"Is she going to get better?"

Deciding I should be straight up with him, I explain, "No, she's not. The doctor said she's only going to get worse."

His eyes welling with tears, Manuel looks away for a moment, then asks, "Is Mom going to get sick like Grandma?"

So that's why Manuel's been acting like a little punk, I think. All this time he's not only been worrying about Abuela, but also about Mom. I've wondered about that myself—if Mom is going to get Alzheimer's like Abuela. Only I haven't wanted to voice it. Swallowing hard, I say, "No, *tonto*. Mom's going to be fine."

Manuel sighs with relief. "It's nice having Grandma around. It's just that I get bugged when she gets into my things."

"Yeah, well you need to lighten up on her, she's just sick."

"I will," Manuel promises softly in a voice I've never heard before tonight.

Realizing what a hard-ass I've been with Manuel, I say, "Listen, if you want, I can help you with your homework. You're almost a freshman, and you'll have to get good grades if you want to go to college."

Manuel jerks his head up in astonishment. "I thought you didn't believe in college."

"Yeah, well, maybe I changed my mind." All of a sudden, I can't believe the words that have just come out of my mouth.

"You should study something like nursing. You'd be good at it 'cause you're real patient with Grandma."

"Me a nurse? Guys can't be nurses."

A smile brightens Manuel's face. "That's not what Mr. Moore said in Health Ed. He said more men are studying to be nurses."

"Well, that's not for us Macho Guys," I say, crossing the room to my bed as Manuel chuckles.

"It's almost two o'clock," I say, glancing at my alarm clock. "Time to get some sleep."

Manuel smiles. "Thanks Rudy. And you can listen to my CDs anytime you want."

Unable to sleep, I lie awake thinking about my conversation with Manuel. I think back to the woman at the support group meeting who said her son was flunking ninth grade. Tess, the group facilitator, had told her that Alzheimer's affected the entire family, including the children. Maybe I needed to hang out more with Manuel instead of spending all my free time with Juanita. Besides, Mom's always saying that Manuel looks up to me since I'm the oldest. I guess I never really thought about it until now.

I finally drift off to sleep, and by the time I wake up the next day, Manuel is already sitting up in bed watching the end of the New Year's Day Parade. "It's about time, Sleeping Beauty," he teases.

"*Híjole*," I say, sounding just like Juanita. It's almost eleven o'clock.

"Don't sweat it," Manuel says, reminding me that Mom always lets us sleep in on holidays.

After I've showered and dressed, I head downstairs to the kitchen with Manuel. We find a note on the table next to a plate of steamed tamales from Mom saying that they've taken Amá with them to visit their *compadre* Juan. I'm secretly pleased because that way I can spend some time with Manuel.

"You want to play videogames?" I ask Manuel as we sit down to eat.

"Aren't you going with Juanita?"

"She's spending the day at Maya's. Besides, I was with her last night. A guy needs a break."

Just then, the phone rings, and Manuel hurries to answer it. After a few moments, I hear him explain, "Sorry, Jordan. I can't. Me and my brother are hanging out today. I'll call you later."

Satisfied, I bite into another tamal, wishing it were a cheeseburger instead. As Manuel sits down to finish eating, he says, "That was Jordan. He wanted me to go over, but I told him I couldn't."

"You better watch out for that little punk. I hear he's always getting into trouble."

For once, Manuel doesn't get defensive. He shrugs, "Jordan's okay. He doesn't do drugs if that's what you think."

"How do you know that?"

"Come on, Rudy, everyone at school knows who smokes pot. Jordan's not like that."

I want to lecture him on choosing better friends, but I decide to drop it. We go into the living room, and I challenge Manuel to a game of *NBA Live*. Then we play his new *Guitar Madness* until I feel like I need some exercise, so I invite Manuel to shoot some real hoops outside.

At the apartment playground, we play several rounds of one-on-one and Manuel ends up beating my butt. "Not bad," I tell him, catching my breath.

His face beaming, Manuel says, "I want to try out for the junior varsity team next year."

"Oh, yeah? Bodybuilding is my thing, but anytime you want to shoot around, just let me know. It's good exercise for my muscles."

Nodding, Manuel grins as I flex my arm at him.

When we get back to the apartment, Juanita calls from Maya's house to wish me a Happy New Year. She seems surprised that I hung out with Manuel all day until I tell her about what happened last night. "I'm glad you listened to him," Juanita compliments me.

"Hey, baby," I quickly exclaim. "I told you I was a sensitive guy!" I can hear Maya laughing in the background as Juanita repeats my comment to her.

TWENTY-TWO

Professor Sonia Gonzales

The moment I awoke, I thought about calling Mom. Staring at the exquisite engagement ring on my finger, I knew I wanted to tell Mom about last night even if she wouldn't understand. Glenn's proposal had come as a complete surprise. We were at the San Martín Inn where we'd gathered with some of Glenn's associates to bring in the New Year when he proposed, handing me the small box. Staring into Glenn's loving eyes, I'd whispered yes, flooded by memories of the solitary years since my divorce from Armando. I wasn't about to let love get away from me now. Maya would have to understand.

Impulsively reaching for the phone, I listened while it rang several times before the nurse finally answered. Then I waited patiently until Mom's voice came on the line. In the final stages of Alzheimer's, she had reverted to speaking entirely in Spanish. "Mom, it's Sonia, your daughter. Happy New Year," I said in my best Spanish.

"Where are you?"

"I'm here in California."

"When did you get here?" Mom asked, and I felt a surge of happiness feeling as if Mom knew I was her daughter. Only this feeling was short-lived when she began to babble about something I couldn't understand. My eyes magnified with tears, but I forced myself to continue.

"Mom, Glenn and I are engaged. Last night, he asked me to marry him."

"When are you coming?" Mom asked, her voice agitated. "I want to go home."

I felt the crushing weight on my chest. "I'll be there in an hour," I lied.

"I'll wait for you," Mom mumbled, her voice sounding lighter.

Rubbing the left side of my chest with my free hand, I whispered, "I love you, Mom."

Her words came out garbled as she tried to repeat "I love you."

As I hung up the phone, I burst into tears at the thought of Mom sitting in the reception area waiting for someone to come by for her. After a few minutes of crying, I calmed down, realizing that by now, Mom had forgotten our conversation. Her memory is gone, I reminded myself going into the bathroom to splash some water on my eyes.

As I stepped back into the bedroom, the phone started to ring. It was Sandy wondering where I'd been last night she'd called to wish me a Happy New Year. "Did Glenn take you out? I couldn't get Frank to budge," she complained.

"Yes, we went dancing at the San Martín Inn."

"Your voice sounds weird. Are you all right?" Sandra abruptly asked.

"I'm fine," I sighed. "Just a little sad. I called Mom, and she barely made sense."

"I'm sorry, Sonia. Alzheimer's is one of the most difficult diseases to cope with, and it's hardest on the family."

"Yes, I know. It's pure hell."

There was a moment or two of silence. "Sonia, are you sure you're all right?"

I drew in a long breath. "Yes, I'll be fine. Oh, Glenn proposed last night."

"Congratulations! It's about time. Have you told Maya?"

"Not yet, but I'll tell her today. Glenn's coming over for dinner. But I'm a bit nervous about how she'll react."

"You have nothing to worry about," Sandy advised. "Maya likes Glenn. Besides, she's come a long way since your divorce from Armando."

After we hung up, I thought about what Sandy had said. Maybe Maya was ready to hear the news of my engagement.

I was in the kitchen having my second cup of espresso when Maya walked into the room looking cute and sassy in a short skirt that reminded me of one I used to wear when I was that age. "Happy New Year," I said, giving her a hug. "How was the party?"

"It was cool. We danced a lot. What's for breakfast?" she asked, opening the refrigerator.

"You're on your own. I'm about to start cooking the ham for our holiday dinner."

Pouring herself a bowl of Cheerios, Maya joined me at the table. She shrieked when she saw the small diamond on my finger. "Mom, is that what I think it is?"

Holding out my hand so that she could examine my engagement ring, I confessed, "Glenn proposed last night."

"It's beautiful," Maya admitted. "I'm going to make Tyrone get me a huge diamond ring when we get engaged."

Smiling, I asked. "I hope this is okay with you?"

"It's cool. I like Glenn." Her brown eyes clouding, Maya sighed, "I know you and Dad will never get back together, especially now that he's with what's-her-face."

Hours later, Glenn appeared at the door carrying a bottle of his favorite Chilean wine. He was wearing a turquoise green sweater that made his eyes turn a darker shade of green. After a quick kiss, I invited him into the kitchen where Maya was busy setting the table. The minute she saw him, Maya offered her congratulations. Grinning, Glenn said, "Thanks, Maya. I'm glad I have your approval."

"She's all yours! Anyway, I'll be graduating soon and leaving for Stanford."

"I'm not that hard to be around," I chuckled.

"Oh, yeah? If you like Attila the Hun!" Maya answered.

Laughing, Glenn replied, "Guess I better learn how to hunt."

Soon we were all seated at the table enjoying my baked ham and parsley potatoes. I had also prepared some homemade red chile for the occasion. When Glenn asked about it, I confessed, "It's Mom's recipe. She and my aunts used to make red chile all the time when I was growing up in New Mexico."

"Grandma used to make the best chile," Maya exclaimed as I described boiling the chiles in water like they did in New Mexico, then grinding them in the blender.

"Have you called your mom?" Glenn asked as I wiped away a tear.

Drawing in a long deep breath, I described my conversation with Mom in the morning. "I know she'll only get worse and there's nothing I can do about it."

"You've done everything you can," Glenn said, squeezing my hand.

Maya suddenly rose to her feet. "I want to propose a toast to the coolest future stepdad anyone could ask for!"

"I'll toast to that!" Glenn smiled and as we raised our glasses in the air, he added, "*¡Colitas arriba!*"

"That's gross," Maya said, but I couldn't help but laugh at Glenn's favorite toast.

After dinner, Maya went off to get ready for her date with Tyrone while Glenn and I went into the family room. We were enjoying the New Year's concert on PBS when my cell phone rang. "Sonia, it's me again. Listen, I was watching the local news, and they announced a Memory Walk this Saturday. It's at Lakeside Park. Thought you might be interested."

"Yes," I answered, remembering I had read about it in the Alzheimer's Association Newsletter.

"It's an important event to bring awareness to the disease as well as to raise funds. Memory Walks are held all over the nation, and Latino families are starting to get more involved. There's even a *Familias Latinas* in the L.A. area. So what do you say?"

"I think it's a very good idea."

Hanging up, I told Glenn about the Memory Walk. "I've heard of them," he said. "They've had several in San Martin. Sounds like it's worth checking out."

TWENTY-THREE

Professor Sonia Gonzales

On Saturday, Glenn arrived at eight-thirty a.m. to drive me to the Memory Walk at Lakeside Park. A few minutes later, Tyrone pulled up in his car with Rudy, Juanita, and Manuel. According to Maya, it had taken some major "sweet talking" to convince Tyrone to attend the Memory Walk, but Rudy had offered no resistance, asking if he could bring his brother along. Maya had told me about Manuel crying in front of Rudy a few nights ago. I knew this was Rudy's way of trying to help Manuel.

Lakeside Park was the ideal place for the Memory Walk. It was circled by majestic rolling hills and bordered by a huge lake. There were a number of trails leading up into the hills. Lakeside Park was the most frequented park in Laguna, where countless events such as the yearly Arbor Day celebration took place. Only last month, Sandra and I had gone there for a large protest march against the war in Iraq.

Driving into the park, we followed the signs that directed us toward the children's play area where a colorful welcome banner had been placed to greet this year's participants in the walk. The parking areas near the main area were completely full, so we turned back and parked near the entrance. People were still arriving for the event. As we gathered together and began walking, I asked Rudy how his parents were coping with his grandmother's illness. Frowning, Rudy answered, "Not good. I invited Mom to come today, only she wouldn't. But I'm really glad Manuel came."

Agreeing with him, I glanced at Manuel, who was deep in a conversation about basketball with Glenn.

We arrived at the welcome banner and continued past the swings toward the central area, where a variety of booths with canopies had been set up for the different sponsors. There were booths representing long-term insurance companies, as well as local organizations like the Seaside Assisted Living Center or the Presbyterian Daycare Center where I had attended the Alzheimer's support group meeting a week ago. I was surprised to see a booth by Laguna Junior College where they were giving out information on medical degree programs in caring for the elderly.

"Look, there's KUVO! That's my fave radio station!" Maya shouted, pulling Tyrone to their booth. Manuel eagerly followed them while Juanita took Rudy with her to the Laguna Junior College booth.

Glancing around, I noticed the diverse crowd that was quickly filling up the park. There were young couples with small children, clusters of teenagers and middle-aged couples with elderly family members.

As Maya and her friends returned to our side, Manuel pointed to a young man with flaming red hair who was posting signs with directions to the bathrooms, saying, "There's my friend Zach from school."

We continued on past the cotton candy and popcorn machines. A small petting zoo had been set up to keep the children occupied. I was pleased to see the face-painting booth sponsored by Nu Alpha Kappa, the new Latino fraternity at Laguna University. I waved to Enoch, a former student from last quarter, who was busy painting the face of a young boy.

Approaching the Walkers check-in line, Maya paused to greet several classmates from Roosevelt who were busy directing people and answering questions. We waited in line until a young man named Steve, who was also a student at Roosevelt, checked our names off the computer printout. When he was finished, I handed him a small envelope. "We would like to make this donation."

Steve thanked me, handing each of us a complimentary ticket for the pancake breakfast. "Where can we get one of those cool T-shirts you're wearing?" Maya asked, and Steve pointed toward the booth sandwiched in between Donny's Drugstore and Dell Computers.

Before we separated, we agreed to meet back at the pancake lines, which were already forming at the kiosk. On the way there, Glenn and I stopped at the Memory Quilt Booth to admire the 10" x 12" squares with names and photos of people who had been stricken with a form of Alzheimer's. "It reminds me of the AIDS quilt," I said, thinking back to the day Sandra and I had gone to see it at the university. It was one of those moments I'd never forget.

Glenn squeezed my shoulder. "Come on, let's go eat. I'm starved."

The smell of pancakes and sausage welcomed us as we entered the breakfast area. There was a jazz band assembling on the kiosk, and the tables were already beginning to fill up with the hungry participants. We were approaching the front of the line when Maya and Juanita returned with Rudy and Tyrone. "Where's Manuel?" I asked, noticing their Memory Walk T-shirts.

"He's helping his friend Zach," Rudy explained.

Once our food was served, we hurried to find a vacant table near the back. As we ate, we were serenaded by jazz sounds. "Man, they could use some *norteñas*," Rudy said.

We were almost finished eating, when a small middle-aged woman with delicate features went up to the microphone and introduced herself as Meg Campbell, this year's Memory Walk organizer. After welcoming everyone, she announced that it was time to gather at the park entrance for the forty-minute walk around the lake and its trails. "I think I'll sit this one out," Tyrone said, but Maya locked arms with him, insisting he wasn't going to flake out on her.

"Don't be a *huevón,*" Rudy scolded, and we all chuckled at his humorous choice of Spanish.

We were walking back to the park entrance when Manuel caught up with us.

"Have you eaten?" Juanita asked him.

"Yeah. Zach and I got there just as they were putting away the food," Manuel answered, moving next to Rudy.

Arriving at the park entrance, I recognized the local TV station that was setting up to film the beginning of the march. A number of volunteers wearing yellow arm bands were already directing the participants into one long line. Waving at one of the volunteers, Rudy said, "That guy's in my weight training class."

Lining up, there were teams composed of six to eight people with individual team captains. Each of the team captains wore a cap with a special designation referring to their team motto. Some of the teams were made up of individual families who carried signs bearing the name of a loved one who had died from Alzheimer's. There were also family members who were marching with relatives who had been stricken with the disease.

As we began the march, voices rang out with chants and songs. I felt uplifted by the energy emanating from the group as we marched around the lake and through the marshlands. From there, we entered the longest trail that led up to the highest mountain. The crowd remained jubilant, but as we reached the end turning around, the chants began to dwindle.

Back at the central kiosk, we were greeted by the sounds of a victory march song. As we headed for an empty table to rest, Maya said, "Mom, we're leaving now. We're gong to the beach."

"Yeah, I'm exhausted," Tyrone groaned and Glenn laughed, telling him he needed to get in shape.

"Not me," Rudy confessed, flexing the muscle on his right arm at Juanita, who ordered him to quit bragging.

Manuel quickly asked Rudy if he could stay behind to help Zach with the cleanup. "His parents will give me a ride home," he explained.

Rudy nodded in agreement and as Manuel left to join his friend, I turned to Rudy and thanked him for coming on the Memory Walk. "It was fun," Rudy grinned. "My mom would've liked it."

Once we were alone again, we focused our eyes on the stage as Meg walked up to the microphone. Thanking the audience for their participation in this year's Memory Walk, Meg invited last year's King and Queen onstage. They were greeted by loud cheers and a huge round of applause. Next, Meg announced the names of this year's new King and Queen. The audience applauded loudly as the exultant couple was crowned. After that, Meg summoned several of her assistants to give out prizes. Gold and platinum awards were handed out to the local companies who had contributed the most money to the event. Certificates with prizes attached to them were then distributed to the teams and individuals who had raised the most money. The prizes, which had been donated by local businesses, ranged from weekend stays at popular central coast spa resorts to smaller gifts of therapeutic massages or bath products. Meg closed the event by reminding the audience about the need to continue to raise awareness about Alzheimer's.

As Glenn drove out of Lakeside Park, I felt the urge to call Mom again. "Sonia, is that a good idea?" Glenn asked. "Remember how depressed you were the last time you called her?"

Ignoring Glenn, I reached inside my purse for my cell phone and dialed the Sage Nursing Home. After a short wait, I heard Mom's voice. "Mom, it's me, Sonia," I explained.

"Sonia?"

"Yes, Mom, your daughter. It's Sonia."

When Mom tried to speak, the words tumbled out in incoherent phrases like the babbling of a child. My heart hammering, I said, "Mom, I called to tell you how much I love you and miss you."

I listened sadly as Mom tried to say she loved me, only the words were incoherent. My eyes moist, I repeated, "I love you, Mom. I'll come see you soon."

TWENTY-FOUR

Rudy

As I wave goodbye to Maya and Tyrone, I notice the tall balding man who is at the front door talking with Mom. I walk up to them, and Mom introduces me to Mr. Hines. "Here, you can have one too," he says, handing me one of the flyers he has given Mom. Looking closely at it, I realize it's about a man who has disappeared. There's a picture of him on the flyer, and he doesn't even look that old.

"What happened?" I ask, following Mom inside the apartment.

Shaking her head slightly, Mom answers, "*Ay, hijo*, this man, Jim Thorpe, he disappeared from his home two nights ago. He has Alzheimer's. His family hasn't been able to find him. *Pobre familia*. They're posting flyers everywhere. I heard it on the news. Guess they're starting to worry he might be dead or even kidnapped."

Suddenly, I feel pinpricks on my back. "Where's Abuela?"

Pointing toward the patio, Mom answers, "She's out back watering her plants. Where's Manuel?"

"He stayed with a friend from school to help clean up. Don't worry. They're bringing him home."

Mom's next question catches me by surprise. "How was that walk?"

"You mean the Memory Walk? It was good. There were a lot of people there, Some even took their relatives who are sick like Abuela."

Mom looks as if she is about to make another comment, but we're interrupted when Dad enters the room. Complaining because of the high gasoline prices, he asks if there's anything to eat. "I'm making *caldo*," Mom, says, moving toward the kitchen before we can finish our conversation.

When Dad invites me to watch the Clippers game with him, I shake my head, insisting I'm a Lakers fan. Then I head upstairs to my bedroom where I stare at Manuel's unmade bed. "He's still a pig," I mumble under my breath picking up my Cucaracha comic books, For the next hour, I laugh my guts out with Lalo Alcaraz's parodies of La Raza, especially the one where La Migra is holding a raffle in the barrio for Cinco de Mayo.

Half an hour later, Mom calls me downstairs to eat. Taking a seat at the table, I ask Dad if the Clippers beat the Timberwolves, and he shakes his head. "No, but the Lakers will next week."

When Abuela almost burns herself helping Mom heat the tortillas, Mom delicately asks her to sit down and eat, so she does. But now, Abuela begins to drown her food in salt. She abruptly pauses and hands me the salt shaker, saying, "*Está bien picoso*."

When Dad complains that Abuela is crazy, Mom rips him apart with her stare, "Rodolfo, I told you not to talk like that in front of her." Then Mom turns to me, her face softening. "*Hijo*, I was thinking I'd like to go to one of those meetings with you."

"*Órale,*" I blurt out, and Dad instantly scolds me for talking like a *cholo*.

Glancing tenderly at Abuela, who is now tearing her tortilla into tiny pieces, Mom says, "I got scared today when Mr. Hines came. It got me thinking how I wouldn't want anything like that to happen to Amá."

"Who is Mr. Hines?" Dad asks.

Just then, we hear the front door slam and moments later, Manuel walks into the kitchen. His face is ashen, and he's holding onto his stomach. "I've got a bad stomach ache," he groans, slumping down on the chair next to Mom.

"It's from all the junk you eat," Dad scoffs, as Manuel admits they stopped off to eat at Burger King.

"You'll get over it when you clean up the mess you left in the bedroom," I tell him sarcastically.

Annoyed, Manuel gives me one of his "Don't mess with me" looks as Abuela rises from the table, saying, "*Hijo*, I know what will make your stomachache go away."

We all watch as Abuela moves to the kitchen cabinet and takes out the baking powder. Handing it to Manuel, she says, "This will make you feel better."

"Are you trying to kill me?" Manuel asks while Dad pretends not to laugh.

"*Ay,* Amá," Mom sighs. "That's not baking soda—it's baking powder!"

On his feet, Manuel mutters, "I'm going to lie down."

Now I turn to Mom and ask, "Do you really want to go with me to an Alzheimer's meeting?"

"Yes, *m'ijo*—I do."

"*Órale*—I mean great," I reply, noticing Dad's approving glance.

After we're done eating, I go back to my room where I find Manuel lying on his bed watching *Hip-Hop Jams*. His bed is still unmade, but at least he's picked up his dirty clothes. "How's your *panza*?" I ask.

"Better. Abuela's really out of it, isn't she?"

"Yeah, I know. Listen, Mom actually said she wants to go to an Alzheimer's support group meeting with me. How about you?"

"Yeah, why not? Today was cool," Manuel states as Mom cracks the door open to tell me Maya is on the phone.

Surprised, I go back downstairs and pick up the receiver. "Hey, what's up?"

"My mom wants to talk with you. She has a surprise for you."

Seconds later, Professor Gonzales comes on the line. "Rudy, I know how worried you and your mom are about your grandmother getting lost again, so I went online and ordered an identification bracelet for her. It'll be here within a week. I'll have Maya give it to you."

"Thanks, Professor Gonzales, that's really nice of you."

"You're very welcome."

"Guess what! My mom said she wants to go to an Alzheimer's meeting next time we go. Manuel too."

"Terrific," Professor Gonzales exclaims as I tell her about the man that's missing and the impression it made on Mom.

"It really scared her, but in a good way." Then, pausing for a moment, I say, "You know, I was thinking maybe I'd take some classes at Laguna Junior College when I graduate, maybe in the healthcare field. I think I might like helping people who are sick like Abuela."

"That's a wonderful idea. And I know a counselor there that you can talk to about receiving financial aid."

"Yeah, Juanita mentioned that too."

After we hang up, I'm about to climb the stairway when Abuela calls me into the living room where she's looking through her pictures again. "Look, Manuel," she says in Spanish, her eyes lighting up like two giant candles. "It's your grandfather, Rodolfo, when he was young. You look a lot like him."

Then Abuela begins to show me her photographs and although I've seen them many times before, I pretend they're all new to me. When Abuela pauses at her wedding day photo and begins to repeat the story about the night my grandfather proposed to her, I recognize how important it is to have Abuela living with us. For the very first time, I realize that Abuela's story is *my* story.

GLOSSARY

abuela/o—grandmother/grandfather.

abuelita—my dear grandmother.

abuelitos—grandparents.

ahijada—goddaughter.

Amá—mother.

Apá—father.

apúrate—Hurry up!

ay, hijo—Oh, son.

barrio—neighborhood.

¡bien trucha!—That's great; swell!

bisabuela—great grandmother.

caldo—soup.

calzones—underwear.

capirotada—type of Mexican bread pudding that is generally traditional for Lent.

chale—No way!

champurrado—a type of atole or Mexican hot chocolate.

chanclas—slippers; sandals.

chismosa—a gossip.

cholo—contemporary Chicano youth who dresses distinctively and rebels against mainstream culture.

Cinco de mayo—An important celebration in Mexican history that commemorates a victory over the French during the Battle of Puebla in 1862.

¡colitas arriba!—Bottoms up!

comadre—a female protector; close family friend; a relative of mutual consent, which may not be by blood.

compadre—a male protector; close family friend; a relative of mutual consent, which may not be by blood.

Cómetelo, hijo. Es saludable—Eat it, son. It's healthy.

corrido—a ballad or type of song that was popularized during the Mexican Revolution.

El Gordo y la Flaca—a popular Spanish-language television talk show hosted by Raúl de Molina, El Gordo, and Lili Estefan, La Flaca.

El Rey de los Pedos—the King of Farts.

enchilado—spicy.

en la calle—On the streets.

es Laura, tu mamá—It's Laura, your mother.

está bien picoso—It's very spicy.

ésta es su casa—This is your house.

está gordito—He's chubby.

están feas—They're ugly.

¿estás loca?—Are you crazy?

estás bien grande—You've really grown.

es un tiburón—It's a shark.

hierbabuena—mint.

hijo—son.

¡híjole!—Wow!; My goodness!; Oh my gosh!

huélelo—Smell it.

huevón—a lazy person.

La campesina—The Peasant Woman.

La Raza—Race, lineage, family; La Raza is a concept that includes all Latinos regardless of nationality; literally, "the race of Spanish-speaking people."

La Migra—popular term used to refer to the INS or Immigration and Naturalization Service.

Los Lonely Boys—Grammy award-winning musical group from San Angelo, Texas, whose musical style combines a variety of sounds with Tejano music.

Los Tigres del Norte—one of the most prominent award-winning Mexican groups that has popularized Norteño music in the United States.

Los Tres Reyes Magos—The Three Kings who visited Jesus in Bethlehem.

lucha libre—refers to all forms of professional wrestling in Spanish-speaking areas.

manzanilla—chamomile.

masa—dough.

MEChA—Movimiento Estudiantil Xicano de Aztlán; an early student organization that was formed during the Chicano Civil Rights Struggle of the 1960s.

menudo—a traditional Mexican dish made with tripe.

m'ija/o—the contraction of "my daughter/son."

m'ijita/o—the contraction of "my little daughter/son."

mole—a type of sauce that consists of all kinds of chiles mixed with spices and unsweetened chocolate.

mosco—derived from the word "mosca," which means a fly.

no sé, hija—I don't know, daughter.

norteña/norteñas—regional Tex-Mex music that encompasses regional ensembles and their particular styles.

órale—Hey! Okay! All right!

padrino—godfather.

pan dulce—Mexican sweet bread.

panza—stomach.

panzón—big-bellied; fatso.

pendejo—idiot; fool; a stupid person

pero todavía eres una flaquita como tu mamá—But you're still skinny like your mother.

pobrecito—You poor thing.

pobre familia—That poor family.

prima/o—female cousin; male cousin.

primos—cousins; plural form of both genders.

¡qué bueno!—That's good.

¿qué pasó, hija?—What happened, hija?

¡qué suave!—That's great.

qué vergüenza—How embarrassing; what a shame.

quinceañera—a traditional Mexican celebration when a girl turns fifteen.

rancheras—a genre of traditional Mexican music played by Norteño or Banda groups.

reggaeton—popular form of urban music with Latino youth which blends reggae, hip-hop and a wide variety of musical sounds.

Rodolfo, ven acá—Rodolfo, come here.

reumas—rheumatism.

Sábado Gigante—a popular Saturday night variety show hosted by Don Francisco.

té de manzanilla—chamomile tea.

telenovelas—Spanish soap operas.

tío—uncle.

tía—aunt.

tías/tíos—plural form of aunts and uncles.

tonto—dummy.

vámonos—Let's go.

vayan a pasearse—Go out; go have a good time.

viejas—old ladies.

viejitas—little old ladies

Virgen de Guadalupe—Mexico's most honored patron saint, the Virgin Mary.

ya me voy a la casa—I'm going home now.

y está esperando un niño—And she's expecting a baby.

Ya quiero irme a mi casa. Ya vámonos—I want to go home now. Let's go.

y a llegaron los reyes de Roma—The King and Queen of Rome have arrived.

Gloria L. Velásquez created the Roosevelt High School Series "so that young adults of different ethnic backgrounds would find themselves visible instead of invisible. When I was growing up, there weren't any books with characters with whom I could relate, characters that looked or talked like Maya, Juanita, or Ankiza. The Roosevelt High School Series [RHS] is my way of promoting cultural diversity as well as providing a forum for young people to discuss serious issues that impact their lives. I often will refer to the RHS Series as my 'Rainbow Series' since I modeled it after Jesse Jackson's concept of the rainbow coalition."

Velásquez has received numerous honors for her writings and achievements, such as being featured for Hispanic Heritage Month on KTLA, Channel 5, Los Angeles, an inclusion in *Who's Who Among Hispanic Americans, Something About the Author* and *Contemporary Authors.* In 1989, Velásquez became the first Chicana to be inducted into the University of Northern Colorado's Hall of Fame. The 2003 anthology, *Latina and Latino Voices in Literature for Teenagers* and *Children*, devotes a chapter to Velásquez's life and development as a writer. Velásquez is also featured in the 2006 PBS Documentary, *La Raza de Colorado*. In 2007, she was also included in the award-winning anthology *A-Z Latino Writers and Journalists*. In 2004, Velásquez was featured in "100 History Making Ethnic Women" by Sherry Park (Linworth Publishing). Stanford University recently honored her with "The Gloria Velásquez Papers," archiving her life as a writer and humanitarian.